PRIVATE DISCLOSURES

RALEIGH DAVIS

CHAPTER 1

I should be feeling more than just *this*.

Achieving a lifelong dream ought to be amazing, wonderful. My heart should be racing with pleasure, my head exploding with unrestrained happiness. I shouldn't be able to stop smiling.

My hands are definitely shaking as I press them into the desk surface, steadying me as I sit in the expensive, ergonomic chair that's now mine. Everything in this office is mine, down to the art on the walls and the sculpture in place of a coffee table in the sitting area.

My office has a *sitting area*. That alone should make me as giddy as a hit of helium.

I've come so far from being Hell Boss's assistant. I took a risk, a huge gamble, on six guys I'd only just met. And it's paying off in full today.

But the bubbles in my stomach aren't only from happiness. The quivers in my pulse aren't from exhilaration.

I'm scared.

I'm excited, yes, but also terrified. Is there a word for happy-scared? Because that's what I am.

I've done it, made it to partner in one of the hottest

venture capital firms in Silicon Valley. I've only been dreaming about this, working toward it, for years.

And now I have to actually *do* it. Find companies to invest in, make them successful beyond anyone's expectations. I've earned this partnership, but now I have to keep it.

"Just breathe," I whisper to myself. "One foot in front of the other."

I'm not what you'd expect as a venture capitalist, even by notoriously lax tech-world standards. My style is decidedly retro—my hair curled and set every day, my makeup heavy but perfect, my clothes straight out of the forties or fifties. Sometimes even the sixties if I'm feeling extra sultry.

I save my flapper dresses for when I'm feeling like the bee's knees.

Today my ink-black hair is done in loose Marilyn Monroe waves, my eyeliner is Elizabeth Taylor-thick, and my dress has a crinoline under the skirt and tiny pirate kitties printed on it. Everyone else in the office is in jeans and a T-shirt. Maybe a cardigan or a hoodie tossed on and the outfit finished off with nerd-cool sneakers.

I don't fit in when it comes to clothes, but then I don't want to. And I don't want the companies I invest in to be the usual either. I can make dreams come true, and I'm going to find the dreams that no one else will take a chance on.

I don't think much about my own dreams, not anymore. This exact position was one of them, and now I've done it. As for the others… well, it's best not to dwell on things that can never happen.

There's a soft knock at the door, and then Mark Taylor, another partner in Bastard Capital, pokes his head in.

Mark used to be my boss, but now I'm his equal. That thought makes butterflies of delight take flight in my veins. I love Mark, love all the Bastards, but I love my new job just as much. Even if it does scare me.

"How is it?" he asks.

"Good." Here comes the smile I can't control. "Amazing. I love it."

Mark steps inside. "It looks much better than when Elliot had the place."

That wouldn't be hard to achieve. Elliot preferred law books as decoration, which works when you're Elliot—he's very type A, no frills—but I'm glad he didn't leave any of those books behind.

The art I've put up is close-up pictures of tattoos, the kind of photos where you can't tell at first if you're looking at a painting on canvas or on someone's skin.

Mark is studying the prints with a frown. "Are any of these your tattoos?"

I laugh. "No. I'm not going to hang those on the wall for just anyone to see."

Mark sizes me up, but of course he can't see anything. All my tattoos are carefully placed so they're under my clothes.

"Finn's not so stingy with his," Mark says.

Finn, another partner, isn't stingy with anything. He's got a massive beard, massive muscles, and tattoos over every inch of him.

"Maybe some of those tattoos up there are Finn's." I wiggle my eyebrows.

Taking the bait, Mark leans in, peering at each of them. "These are all too classy," he mutters. His attention swings toward the sculpture in the middle of the room. "I see you stuck with that theme."

"One of Callie's friends made it," I say. "I've loved her work for a while, but I didn't have a place to display it."

"I have to say, you've really made this office your own. I can hardly remember what it used to look like." A gleam comes into his eyes. "So, what companies do you think you'll invest in first?"

Ah, Mark, always the dealmaker. If his girlfriend, January,

didn't drag him away for dates and couple's trips occasionally, he might never talk anything but business.

Mark and January are my doing. Along with Logan reuniting with his wife, Callie; Finn falling for Doc; and Paul getting engaged to Grace. Elliot falling for and running away with Minerva has nothing to do with me, and I'm still somewhat suspicious of her. For good reason.

When it comes to the Bastards of Bastard Capital, I've been their fairy godmother in both business and romance. I get whatever they want at work and whatever they need in their personal lives. Turns out what they all needed were kick-ass women who would stand up to them and stand beside them.

But with all of them paired off, there's no more matchmaking for me to do.

I don't let myself think of Dev, not even the briefest flash. I shiver anyway, my body acting independently of my mind.

"I'm going after underserved markets," I tell Mark.

Back when I worked for Hell Boss, I tried to steer her toward those kinds of things, apps and projects the rest of the tech world was overlooking. She smacked me down quick when I did though. Now I can do whatever I please. A smile tickles my lips at the thought.

"Are you going to tell me now, or do I have to wait until the Monday-morning partners' meeting?"

"Oh, I'm going to make you wait."

"Good. Show us who's in charge." He's laughing as he says it. "We're going to throw a party for you too."

"I don't—"

He shakes his head. "Don't pull that fake-humility crap. You're a partner now; you get a party. Where would you most like to throw the biggest party of the year?"

Oh boy. These guys take their parties seriously. They rented out Alcatraz for Logan's last birthday—yes, *that* Alcatraz—and Paul's family throws *the* charity event to see and be

4

seen at for all of San Francisco society. I could say I wanted to have it in the Louvre, and they'd find a way to make it happen.

Maybe a hotel? San Francisco has its share of luxury hotels. Or the Marines' Memorial Club?

"What about the Presidio Officers' Club?" It's in a charming building, and the Presidio itself is simply lovely.

Mark pulls a face. "It's kind of small. We could only fit, what, two hundred people in there?"

"Two fifty," I say. "But smaller is better. It'll be exclusive, and everyone will be dying to get an invite."

The thought of the most powerful people in Silicon Valley fighting to get into *my* party makes me happier than it should. But I've never claimed to be perfect or even above some pettiness.

"Genius," Mark says. "I'll get Yancy to work on it."

"Oh, I can do it."

Yancy is my replacement as office manager. She's doing a fine job of it, but sometimes there are things I'd do differently, and it… itches at me.

"No." Mark is firm. "I'll do it, because it's not your job anymore. Remember?"

I take a deep inhale. "Okay. I'll leave it to you."

"I promise we won't screw it up." He heads for the door. "Enjoy your new office."

When he's gone, I shake out my hands. All the happy feelings are leaving, and the anxiety is rushing back in. This isn't my first day here, but I'm as wound up as if it were.

I force myself to open a folder filled with prospectuses. I couldn't give Mark any details about the companies I'm going to invest in because I haven't settled on any one start-up yet. I've been too busy moving my office, training my replacement, and signing paperwork to have time to actually look into what I'll be doing from now on.

The first is from a company that looks like every other

start-up in the Valley. A group of men—it's almost always men—bragging about something "paradigm shattering." Lately AI has been all the rage, and these guys of course are using AI. They're also promising way more than they can deliver. I know for a fact the technology they're proposing is at least ten years in the future. And nothing I see makes me believe they've got the talent to make that leap before anyone else.

I set it aside, reach for another one. As I do, I glance at my atrium. I call it mine because I'm the one who planted everything in there, designed where the paths and benches would go, and I'm the one who tends to the plants.

I had an ulterior motive when I set up the atrium. I'm obsessed with orchids. Plain ones, common ones, rare ones, ugly ones, heart-stopping ones. I love them all. They're finicky and tricky and need constant care. Push them even a little bit out of their preferred environment and they punish you by dying. They're also carnivores; beautiful carnivores that consume the very trees they live on.

So I made those beautiful carnivores a perfect environment to live in. The lush greenery, the massive tree trunks, the state-of-the-art climate control is all for them. People come to our offices and ooh and aah over the flashier plants in the atrium but often miss the orchids hiding in the hollows.

I like that. Like that I've made this beautiful thing where the true beauty is difficult and consuming and hidden in plain sight.

And then Dev steps out from behind a fern.

I immediately look away without even thinking about it, as if we're two repelling magnets.

It's been like this since I became partner. Dev not looking at me, me not looking at him. We've been very careful to keep our relationship professional, distant, from the moment I was hired, but it's gone into overdrive the past few weeks.

We could at least look at one another before. Not for very long—I'd get too warm, shaky all over if I held his gaze for more than a moment—but we did it. Now… now there's a wall between us.

His takeover of Corvus, which he did without telling anyone, hasn't helped matters. Dev has always been the one who didn't quite fit in, at least not as well as the others. Things are decidedly strained now.

I don't think he's watching me, but I still feel exposed. Pinned like a squirming butterfly. It's those gold eyes of his. He can wield them like a hammer or like a set of forceps, striking or delicate, however he pleases.

But they never give anything away, those eyes, and that's how it pleases him too.

I wonder what he's doing in the atrium. He never goes in there. The others do, from the partners to the interns, either enjoying lunch or a stroll or simply some quiet time. But not Dev.

I'm unaccountably angry. He avoids the place for years, and now—*now* he decides to invade it? The fucking gall.

I'm also imagining him touching the orchids. His long, strong fingers tracing the delicate petals, fingering the velvet of them. Maybe his hand would trail down a stem, the backs of his fingers slipping over the cool, slick greenery. He might even cup a bloom in his hands, protecting it, shielding it.

I'm not looking at him, but my body is reacting like we've locked gazes for hours. My pulse is out of control, my breasts heavy, my thighs aching. If he meant me to notice him, it's working.

But… I have no idea what point he's trying to make or if he's even trying to make one at all. Perhaps with the Corvus thing and everyone being cool toward him, he needs the warmth of the atrium. Needs the peaceful solitude.

I always thought he had more than enough peaceful solitude within him—he's the most alone man I've ever met—but maybe he doesn't. Not anymore.

With a rustle of paper, I take another prospectus. I also ignore the sensations warring inside my body—it's only instinct, and I'm better than that. Whatever Dev might be feeling, he brought it on himself. He chose to be apart from the Bastards, to be the mysterious one even among his friends. He also chose to go after Corvus entirely on his own. Corvus hurt and attacked people the Bastards love, the people closest to them. But Dev somehow thought only he could take them on.

I've managed to give everyone else at Bastard Capital exactly what they need. But I have no idea what Dev needs.

I don't think he knows either.

CHAPTER 2

The ocean is never quiet here.

It's always sullen, gray, the wind whipping up the sand and driving it across the dunes, the highway, and against the windows of my living room. The picture windows frame Ocean Beach, but it's never a pretty picture. Even when it's sunny—which it almost never is—there's something cold about this beach. Unwelcoming. It doesn't want you to sun yourself here.

I take a sip of wine, cozy inside my living room as the ocean crashes outside. This part of town is sometimes called Lands End, and looking out at this view, it fits. Land, civilization, human habitation should all end here. The sea owns the rest.

Oceanfront property in San Francisco isn't the coveted stuff it is elsewhere in California. My house still cost a pretty penny though. But the Bastards have always been generous with my salary, and my house is proof of that. I've got three bedrooms, a living room with an entire wall of picture windows, a modern kitchen, a garage, and a backyard, all just for me. This much space for one person in the City is the ultimate extravagance.

Now that I'm a partner, I can afford something even

bigger, more luxurious. Somewhere in a more popular neighborhood—there isn't much happening in Lands End beyond a few coffee shops and some restaurants. Oh, and one bar. People don't want to travel this far out, all the way to the end of the N-Judah. Not when there's only the sullen Pacific waiting for them.

I'm going to stay here though. This house suits me. I've spent a lot of time making it into exactly what I want. And the park is only ten blocks away. I fill my weeknights with social events and classes and volunteering. But my weekend days are spent alone, walking through the park.

I swirl the last few sips of wine in my glass. The liquid clings to the sides, running down sluggishly. I know the feeling—I went out with the Bastards tonight to celebrate, ate way too much rich food, then had dessert, washing it down with champagne and wine. It's almost midnight and I'm going to be hurting tomorrow, especially if I don't get to bed soon.

Dev didn't come out with us. When Logan went to ask him, he wasn't in his office. Didn't answer his phone.

I'd say he haunted us with his absence at dinner—which everyone very carefully avoided talking about—but we're missing more than Dev. Elliot left the firm recently, partly because he was ready to do something else and partly because Minerva, the woman he fell in love with, is on the run from the law.

Paul is gone too, moved back to Taipei to run the family business. He and Grace are happy there, but we miss him.

There's still Mark and January, Logan and Callie, and Finn and Doc, but I think all of us noticed something missing tonight. I definitely did. My neck ached from forcing myself not to look at the door every few minutes to see if Dev would come.

It hurt to look and it hurt to not look. But my chest aches most of all, because he never showed.

I sigh and toss back the last of my wine. Enough watching the sea and being melancholy. It's bedtime. Way past bedtime.

I start pulling out my hairpins as I walk to my bedroom, leaving them on various end tables. Since it's only me here, I can set things wherever I want. I'm not messy exactly, but I don't have to be uptight about where things go.

Three bobby pins tinkle as I set them on the table in the foyer. The stairs to my bedroom are just off the entryway, my bed calling to me. I kick off my heels by the door. I should have done that when I walked in, but I was buzzed on food and wine. Carefully I set them on the rack, because a good pair of heels is priceless. And these are Mary Janes in the most sinful shade of red, tied with a massive silk bow.

I straighten up once the heels are safe, curling my toes against the cold tile. I lift up onto the balls of my feet, once, twice, working the kinks out of my feet. Someday I'm going to regret wearing heels so often. But not enough to stop now.

There's a sharp knock at the door. Then another. Hard, insistent.

I spin, my heart slamming into my ribs. Sick adrenaline floods my throat.

The knock comes again, the raps coalescing into a pattern. My heart slows down, down, down until I feel like I'm suspended in honey. I'm both electric and frozen all at once.

I knew *he* would come, somehow. I didn't think it would be right now.

My muscles trembling, I slowly open the door, the wind stealing inside when I do. The weather is vicious tonight. It bites and snaps, and inside me something dark and needy does as well.

Dev stands on my doorstep, the fog collecting wetly in his dark hair as the wind whips it into his eyes. He's only in a jacket, the collar down, and he must be freezing. But if he is, he doesn't show it.

Not even the weather can make him bend.

He says nothing as he waits. But what is there to say? We put something on hold four years ago, and we've come to the point where we need to finish it.

I step back, let him inside. This time when our gazes meet, neither of us look away. This time our gazes lock.

We've been alone before. We've been alone so often it's hardly remarkable when we are. We conduct business, carry on as if nothing is between us.

That lie is shattered by the force of our gazes interlocking.

I have to kiss him. I'd do almost anything to kiss him. I've been holding my breath for him for years, and now I have to breathe or die. Kiss him or die.

We kissed just once before. Back when I was deciding whether to leave my old job and join the Bastards on their crazy adventure. Dev kissed me, and it ruined kisses for me forever.

And then he said it could never happen again since I'd be working for him and he wasn't that kind of asshole.

It made sense at the time. I understood and even appreciated his position. I wanted the job, took the loss of him as the price I'd pay for moving up in the world. If we were fucking each other, it would have been disastrous. I was his subordinate back then and therefore completely off-limits.

But things between us have shifted at work. It's why he's here now.

I'm not his employee anymore. I'm his partner, his equal. And I'm burning for him. A greedy, consuming fire grips me from my head to my toes.

He shrugs out of his jacket, lets it fall to the floor. Two long strides—his legs are magnificent, made for eating up distances, especially the distance between us—and he's reaching for me.

His hands come up, cup my jaw, tilt my face up to his. There's an expression on his face I haven't seen since the last time we kissed: wonder and reverence and openness. He looks awed by me.

His skin is cool from the night air, his scent crisp with salty chill. It's like he's wearing the weather as cologne. A strand of dark hair falls over his brow, a stark contrast to the deep warmth of his golden eyes.

I part my lips as he lowers his head.

And we kiss for the second time.

This kiss is as shocking as the first, but there's also a sense of rightness. Of homecoming. His hands fit my face perfectly, his mouth made for mine.

The need in my core shifts and sharpens. I'm getting the kiss I was desperate for, but my body wants more.

He slides a thigh between mine, his hips cradled in my belly. His erection presses into me, and a pulse of heat and urgency deep inside me answers. My entire body is awash with heat.

I reach for him, settling my hands on his torso, finding my way to the hard muscles of his back, traveling down to the divide between his hips and his ass. He flexes under my hand, thrusting into my belly.

When I moan, he deepens the kiss. It's like falling into light—white-hot, bright, blinding. Like looking directly at the sun, a dangerous temptation.

I've dreamed of this for so long. Waited for it for so long. And it's exactly as I remembered and imagined.

But every fantasy has an end. So does this one.

I know Dev much better now than I did back then. Working together, day in and day out, brings a kind of intimacy as well. Not the kissing kind, but something deeper. He's here and we're together physically, and my body is screaming this is right, inevitable… but my brain knows my body is confused.

I pull away. My hand finds his chest, and I push.

He stumbles backward, confusion wrinkling his brow. "What's wrong?"

I wrap my arms around myself, wishing I had on my heels. It's hard to confront him when I have to look up to him. When the crane of my neck reminds me of how he angled my head to kiss me deeper, harder.

"This isn't happening." I manage to get it out, barely.

His jaw tightens. "I don't understand. We waited years for this. And now it can happen."

"I didn't wait."

He goes very still. "I never asked you to."

He thinks I mean dating, which of course I've done since we kissed the first time. But I mean something very different. He's not my only impossible dream.

"You weren't at dinner tonight." I can't keep the hurt out of my voice. Can't stop remembering how badly I wanted to watch the door, to see him coming through it.

And he never did.

He glances away, almost defensively. "I was busy dealing with Corvus stuff."

"You didn't come into my office today to see how I was. Everyone else did. Paul and Elliot even called." I swore I wouldn't get emotional, but the feelings keep leaking out of my words.

"I… I didn't think about it." His tone is flat.

I close my eyes for a brief moment. One of the most important days of my life, when I achieve everything I've been striving for, and he didn't think about it.

He was busy. With his own stuff.

I open my eyes, make my back stiff and straight. I need to be as unemotional as he is. "You think I'm the same person I was four years ago. That I kept myself in stasis for you."

"That's not true." Finally he shows some vehemence.

"I've watched you over the years." I couldn't stop watching him. Even when it hurt. "And you're... you're even more closed off now. No one ever knows what you're thinking or feeling. No one knows anything about your family or where you came from. If you've had a relationship, none of us knows anything about it."

I thought that maybe I wasn't lucky enough to know those things about him, that once I was trusted enough, he'd tell me. But it turns out no one's trusted enough by Dev. No one knows anything.

He might be ready to kiss me—and more—but he's not ready to be with me. He's not ready to risk his emotions.

"I'm not... I don't expose myself like that," he says through gritted teeth.

"It's not exposure." I lift my hands, trying to explain. "It's having friends, relationships. People you love and who love you. And those guys, the ones at Bastard Capital? They do love you. You really hurt them with the Corvus stuff."

I saw their pain, their betrayal, and I felt it myself. We all worked together so closely for years... but Dev didn't see it that way. He didn't want to be part of our family.

We'd been rejected.

"They understand." His tone is flat again.

"No, they don't. When you were plotting all this, did you ever think of them? Of how they would feel when you revealed you'd been working behind their backs?"

"I couldn't... I couldn't tell anyone, or it might have failed." He's dragging the words out like he can't catch his breath.

"No, you couldn't *trust* them. That killed them to learn that. Because they trusted you. Completely. And you shattered that for... for Corvus?"

I want him to explain it, to justify what he did. Yes, Corvus needed to be taken down, all their nasty programs dismantled, but everyone at Bastard Capital was doing that. He was the only one who had to take them on entirely alone.

He says nothing. He won't look at me. He's closed off again, just like he always wants to be.

When I kissed him four years ago, I found that reserve of his mysterious. Alluring.

Now I see it as a wall that no one can break. What's on the other side would be more than worth it—Dev, open, honest, ready to love—but I'd shatter myself on that wall before it even cracked. I can't sacrifice myself on a hopeless quest even if he's all I ever wanted. Even if this is tearing me apart inside.

Better to hurt now than to struggle and ache for years and still never reach him.

"This wouldn't have worked," I say quietly. I'm staring at the floor because if I meet his eyes, I might still change my mind. His gaze is that powerful for me. "We can't restart something that's doomed to fail."

He raises his head, his gaze meeting mine. He looks angry, wounded. "Then why did you kiss me?"

"Because after four years of your silences, I deserved something." It comes out smaller, meaner than I meant it, but I don't want to admit that I'm weak. That I had to give in to the urge to touch him, kiss him, even though I already knew it could go nowhere.

I sound small and mean because I feel small and mean. And achy and devastated.

He heads for the door then. With one long arm, he snags his discarded jacket. The stiffness in him, the pain, tears at me in spite of my resolve.

"I don't know what you need," I say frantically. "I can figure out almost anyone else—their hopes, their desires. But you… I don't know what it is you want."

He stops for a brief moment but doesn't turn around. Then he leaves without another word.

CHAPTER 3

Anjelica's wrong. It's not a question of what I want; it's what I need. And I finally know exactly where what I need is.

It's hidden somewhere in the massive array of files and data that Corvus holds, and I just have to find it. Except that searching their archives for what I want is like looking for a single sheet of paper within every single library in the United States. Public, private, and university libraries. Every book you can think of, and I'm in search of one sheet.

Once I find it, I'm turning my attention back to Anjelica. She's wrong about me, and she's wrong about us. I'll prove it to her. Not that my attention is ever truly off her—she's always in the back of my mind, a shape always at the corner of my vision. Even when she's not here, she's here for me.

I'm in my office, scrolling through file directories on my computer. It's tedious work that a search program would be better suited for, but all the algorithms I've written to search the archives have come up empty.

There's always artificial intelligence, and I'll need it for the next search programs I design, but for now I can look with my own two eyes. It's midnight on a Thursday, and I've got nothing else to do.

Thursdays are Anjelica's painting class. It used to be her

dance class night, but the school promoted her to instructor several months ago, and now she teaches on Tuesday night.

She thinks I don't notice her, but she couldn't be more wrong. All I've done over the past few years is notice her. More than notice—I've been damn near obsessed with her, not that I could show it. And then she made partner and I thought...

I thought wrong is what I did.

I keep scrolling through files, automatically cataloging the names as my mind wanders off to more interesting subjects. I wish Minerva were here—the expertise of a Corvus employee would help.

Now that I own the company, I can call on any Corvus employee I like, have them in my office in a few minutes. But I can't trust any of them with this task.

I can't really trust Minerva either, but I could frame it in a way that she wouldn't understand what I was really looking for. Doesn't matter though since she's off with Elliot, working to clear her name.

Finn and Doc could help me with the AI. But I don't like the idea of that. I've been searching for this for so long I have to be the one to find it. No help, not from anyone.

I couldn't explain that to Anjelica. It's hard for me to explain myself and my reasoning to most people, but when it comes to her...

My fingers slow, then stop scrolling. I fell in love with her the moment I saw her.

It was an accident actually. We'd just gotten a final accounting of how much we all made through my miraculous stock algorithm, and it was a lot. Like, a shit ton, especially for a bunch of dudes working out of a garage. When I saw the numbers, I had to go outside for a second because my brain wasn't grasping it.

Our lives were upended, literally overnight. We had fuck-you money and then some. Except… what we were supposed to do now?

I was pacing in front of the garage, trying to clear my head. And then Anjelica came walking down the street in those shoes that hurt her feet. There was something about how she kept going, pretending that everything was fine… I was gone. My heart jumped out of my chest, searching for her hands to catch it. It never came back.

I've scoffed at ridiculous shit like that before, and I still do, but I can't deny what happened. She was so… so different. She was hiding in plain sight—still is—and my heart immediately recognized it. Recognized her.

I don't deal well with people, but I knew I couldn't simply walk up and declare my love. That's stalker shit.

So I waited for her to come to me. We walked together to her bus stop twice. And we talked. Everything about her was so bright, so bursting with color. I was enthralled.

And then she decided to accept the Bastards' job offer. I didn't speak for or against it. I said nothing at all, and they didn't think it odd. I could have stopped them, told them that I loved her and we couldn't hire her.

I didn't. Because I might have fallen just like that for her, but she didn't feel that way about me. She was attracted to me, sure, but it wasn't deeper than that. She had a right to say yes or no to the job offer without my screwing it up.

When she did say yes, our personal relationship was done. To have power over someone and use it to manipulate them into being intimate with you…

I shudder. No, I could never do that.

In the end, we made the right choice. Anjelica was perfect as our office manager. She'll be perfect as a partner.

I just thought that now we might… but I was wrong. She thinks I'm not ready. I am, have been for years, but convincing her will take some planning. Because I don't understand why she stopped, not really. Her reasoning made no sense to me. Of course I didn't tell anyone about my plans —that's why they worked. They should all be happy about what I did, not pissed at me.

It doesn't hurt. I'm used to being alone. It's pretty much all I've ever known, at least until I found the Bastards. No, it's not hurt. More of a hollowness.

I start to scroll again. What's hiding in these files will help. When I find it, the hollowness will be filled. Or at least papered over.

The night custodian passes my office with his cleaning cart and gives me a wave. I wave back.

"Stopping for lunch soon?" It might be odd to think of midnight as lunchtime, but Alfred and I have flipped schedules compared to the normal world.

"Yep. You?"

I shake my head. "I've got too much to do. There're leftover sandwiches in the fridge if you want some."

Anjelica used to order all the food, but it's Yancy's job now. She orders from the same places Anjelica did, but somehow it doesn't quite taste the same.

"Thanks. I'll try one." Alfred hesitates. "You sure you don't want to take a break?"

The concern in his voice makes me wonder what I look like. I've been spending the days doing my usual work—finding new start-ups to invest in, watching over the ones I've already invested in, and the more shadowy work I do. At night for the past few weeks, I've been going through the Corvus files. I sleep of course, but not much.

"I'm all right." I'm not, not really, but Alfred doesn't want to know that.

He points to the atrium, shrouded in darkness beyond the glass wall of my office. "I heard that noise in there again. Like a sprinkler was overpressure."

I sigh. "Thanks. I'll look at it."

Alfred heard the noise first last week and told me about it. So I went into the atrium to search out what it could be.

It was the first time I've ever been inside there. The atrium is Anjelica's. It's so powerfully, intimately hers that I couldn't possibly go inside. I can't believe other people simply walk in, stroll around, sit for a while. It's like rifling through her brain. Or maybe her heart.

But there was something wrong in there, and I wanted to see if I could fix it. I never did find the source of the noise. But the orchids... My God, the orchids. Hidden in every hollow, every corner, waiting to be found. Hiding in plain sight. It was almost too much.

I heard the noise last week, during the day. I went in, searching for it, and Anjelica caught me. I felt like she saw me staring at her or something. Watching her through those glass walls when she couldn't see me, hiding in the paradise she created.

I left before I found the noise. No one else seems to have heard it. I should have called the landscaping guys, let them deal with it, or even told Anjelica, but I wanted to fix it myself. I know a thing or two about irrigation. It could be done without anyone knowing something was wrong.

"It's a strange noise," Alfred says. "I know it's probably the sprinklers, but it sounds like an animal moaning. Or screaming."

I get up out of my chair. "It's just the water in the pipes. Save a sandwich for me, will you?"

Alfred disappears down the hall, and I walk through the door in the glass wall to the atrium. Since I never use it, the hinges squeal as it opens.

Faintly there comes a high-pitched whine. The call of a pipe about to break.

The light from my office gives just enough illumination for me to see the pathway. I cock my head, trying to home in on the noise. As the door shuts behind me, I'm wrapped up completely in the heat and humidity. The HVAC system pushes a gentle breeze through the room, making the palm fronds shiver.

An orchid that looks like a bird in flight perches on one of the branches above my head. Two more nestle in a tree hollow at my right elbow, tight buds dotting the new stems.

The noise gets higher, then starts to sputter. I turn my head, listen hard. Maybe it's by Finn's office.

I take several steps in that direction, still listening. The pauses between the sputters grow longer and longer... and then the noise dies.

Damn. It's probably not going to start up again anytime soon. It's like the noise doesn't want to be caught.

But still, it might. So I find the nearest bench and sit. In the dark, some of the power of the foliage and colors is lost. But the fragrance is all the more potent.

I tilt my head back, fill my lungs. The scent of the orchids is so full I can taste it, pollen sprinkling over my tongue. The warmth settles into my tired muscles, helped along by the humidity. Slowly, inch by inch, my body unlocks, settles.

I start to drift between sleep and wakefulness. My mind rambles off on various larks—recalling my schedule for tomorrow, going through the Corvus files, imagining a beach. Waves and heat.

"Dev?"

My eyes snap open. Anjelica is there, in the atrium.

She's in casual clothes—a T-shirt, yoga pants—and her hair is down, her face bare. The shirt clings to her breasts, and the pants outline her curves in mouthwatering detail.

I close my eyes for a moment. I did not need that image, which is going to haunt my dreams for a while. For forever.

"Are you okay?" she asks. "What are you doing here?"

I'm not sure if she means the atrium or the office. I rise up off the bench, run a hand through my hair. "I was working. There was a noise, like a sprinkler was breaking."

"Oh." She has her keys clutched tightly in her hand. "I don't hear anything."

I have to look at anything but her. This is much too raw. "It's gone now. It only comes occasionally. Why are you here? Is something wrong?"

"There's, uh…" She points to the main door of the atrium. "…a remote alarm that goes off if the heat or humidity is off. Sends a notification to my phone."

I frown at the panel she's pointing at. All I can see of it is a small green LED. "No alarm sounded here."

"I think it's malfunctioning. The readings all look correct to me—I don't know why I got an alert."

"Well, the sensors might be malfunctioning. Do you have—"

She holds up a small temperature and humidity meter from her pocket. "I checked with this in case the sensors were broken."

Right. Of course she would be prepared. Of course she wouldn't need any help.

"I'll get someone out to look at it," I say. "They can check the sensors and the irrigation system."

She bites her lip. "That's okay. This is my thing. I'd really rather do it myself."

It's the choice I would make. Doing it myself, never letting anyone else in. Yet it still hurts me when she says it.

This is what she meant when she said I hurt everyone with the Corvus takeover. That I should have trusted them.

I understand the pain, but… but I'm not sure how to make things right. How to fix what's broken between me and the Bastards, what's broken inside me.

I never got a guide in how to relate to people. How to trust them. It hasn't bothered me—I've done pretty well for myself, and trust isn't exactly necessary for my work. I've learned to cope, and having as much money as I do means people are more than willing to accommodate me.

"Okay," I say. "I understand."

Because I really do. It's one of the few things that I do understand about Anjelica's feelings and needs.

"I mean, I appreciate—" She catches herself, curls her hands into fists. "You're not my boss anymore," she says to herself. When her gaze meets mine, it's resolved. Chilly. "Thanks for the offer. But I'll do it. Don't worry about it."

I'm being dismissed. More kindly than I was at her house, but still dismissed.

I understand that too.

"I'll get back to work then."

There's a flare of something like concern in her eyes as I turn to go, but I don't let myself turn back to make certain. And I don't let myself linger on her, her expressions, or those damn yoga pants.

CHAPTER 4

When my phone rings Monday morning, I pick it up and groan. I really don't have time to answer this, not before my very first partners' meeting.

Well, not my *very* first, but my very first as a partner. I've been getting prospectuses together all weekend and even called in some people for interviews. I've got a portfolio together, filled with start-ups I'm excited about.

And now I get to pitch them to my partners. It's ridiculously exciting.

But I can't ignore this call. Not if I want to keep making progress on my project to fix things with my family.

I hit the Answer button. "Mom. What's up?"

"Anjie, honey. How was your weekend?"

"Fine. I was working."

There's a hiccup of silence. "Oh. Not too much, I hope. Did you have a date?"

Now that we've reconnected, my mother is desperate to hear about the men I'm seeing, to know if there's any chance I'll settle down. Considering how poorly it went the last time they set me up and encouraged me to marry a guy, you'd think she'd have learned her lesson.

"No," I say. Dev kissing me in a way that set fire to my

panties doesn't count. My tossing him out forever doesn't either.

I repeated to myself all weekend that I made the right choice. That I couldn't fix what was wrong with him and it wasn't my job to do so. It became a chant, repeated so often the words lost their meaning.

I did the right thing. But sometimes, in the loneliest parts of my weekend, it felt wrong.

I'm not bringing up any of that with my mother. "Now that I'm partner," I say, "I've got a lot more work."

"That's nice, sweetie. Dad says hi." In the background, I can hear my dad grumbling something. He must be on his way out to the garden. Now that he's retired, he spends most of his days pruning, hunting weeds, and obsessing over his lawn.

"Hi, Dad," I say loudly.

"Oh, he didn't hear you. And now he's gone." Mom sighs. "He's very busy too these days. That one planter by the sycamore tree? You know it."

I don't. They put in the planters after I left. I haven't been home since I graduated from college. I wasn't speaking to my parents for a very long time, so visits were definitely not happening.

Now that we've normalized relations, I'll have to go visit. Someday.

"Yeah," I say absently. She doesn't really care if I know what she's talking about or not. I put the phone between my ear and shoulder and start sorting through my papers.

"That planter started to rot. There was something in the wood, eating it. And now Dad has to tear it out and replace it. I don't think the roses in there can be saved, and he's very upset about it."

I think it's actually Mom who's upset about it—Dad never liked roses because of the thorns and how much water they need. Mom agitated for roses.

That was always the pattern. Dad went for the practical, simple but perfect. Mom wanted the bells and whistles even if they were messy.

"That's too bad." I make a note to send Mom some bare-root roses for Christmas. I should be able to find some rare, spectacular varieties. She'll be the envy of the neighborhood.

"It is. Oh, and you know who offered to help him?"

My throat starts to close, my skin going cold. It's a stupid, teenage reaction, one I should completely be over, but I'm not. I already know exactly who she'll say, and I'm already dreading it.

"Who?" I manage to keep my voice somewhere close to normal.

"Kaleb," Mom says, as if it's just so awesome.

"That's very nice of him." And it is. Kaleb is so kind, to my parents, to his neighbors, his wife and his children. He's got quite the life going for him back home.

My life is good too. It's great. I've got nothing to resent Kaleb for.

"Oh, honey." Mom sighs. "You can't still be upset."

"I'm not." It's true. It's ridiculous to cut off your family, your former friends, all over a man. I've completely gotten past that, which is why I'm talking to Mom right now. I've realized my reaction was wrong, overwrought.

I'm the better person I should have been from the very beginning. And if I still ache for that lost dream I might have had with Kaleb—a husband, children, the intimacy of home overflowing with love—well, that's my problem. Because I went and fell for a guy who could never give me that. If I'd just gotten over Dev properly, let my heart move on…

"I'm happy for him," I say. "I really am. Tell him I said hi and thanks for helping Dad."

Yancy passes by my office, tapping her watch face. Five minutes until the meeting.

I installed a reminder system on all the partners'

computers to prod them into showing up on time—a particularly annoying one in Finn's case—but Yancy is going for a more old-fashioned method. Which is fine. She doesn't have to do everything the exact way I did. As long as everyone's on time to the meeting.

Which includes me.

"Sorry, Mom, but I have to go." And thank goodness.

"All right. Have fun today."

I smile because she makes it sound like I'm off to another day of fifth grade or something. "Thanks. I will."

Miracle of miracles, everyone's on time for the meeting. At least everyone who's still here. Paul's seat is empty, and Elliot's chair has been taken over by Yancy. I suppose she could have my usual seat and I could have used Elliot's, but I've gotten attached to my spot.

Logan is on my right with Mark on the other side of him. Dark circles are under Logan's eyes, but somehow it only makes him more attractive. When it comes to handsomeness, Logan is beyond blessed.

"How's Aurelie?" I ask him.

He groans. "It turns out there's this regression phase babies go through at six weeks. Just when they start to sleep for longer than an hour at time—wham! It's endless crying. Especially at nighttime."

I wince. "That doesn't sound fun."

"I mean, she's still the most beautiful thing in the world," Logan says quickly.

I nod solemnly. "Of course. How's Callie doing?"

"She's so amazing." Logan's expression softens. "I never knew she could be so patient. Even when she's so tired. I'm just in awe."

My heart swells with happy triumph. I knew Logan and Callie would work their problems out and have a happily-ever-after. When they first got together, it was too fast, too soon. I could see that, although I couldn't say anything at the time.

When they broke up and got back together, it was meant to be. I might have helped them along a little bit, but they were made for each other. They just had to grow up and into their marriage.

"It sounds amazing," I say with a smile.

"Come by and see us some night," Logan says. "You can see Aurelie's new trick of holding her head up."

Mark leans over. "I saw it this weekend. It's amazing."

Logan rolls his eyes. "Wait until you have a kid. You're never going to shut up about it."

"I was being serious," Mark says. "I'd never make fun of your kid. You, yes. Your kid, no. Although it is impressive that you manage to keep that massive noggin of yours upright. I guess Aurelie learned it from you."

Finn and I both bust out laughing. Yancy looks like she isn't sure if she should join in. And Dev… Dev's staring down at something on his computer screen, completely oblivious to what's happening around him.

I stop laughing when I see him.

Logan punches Mark on the shoulder, which is the equivalent of a hug for these guys. "Fuck off. And let's get this meeting started." He rubs his hands together. "We have a new partner to haze."

I know they're not actually going to haze me or even really tease me—much—but my palms still go clammy. "So, where do I go in the order now? At the end? Or…"

"You go first," Finn says.

Oh. Okay. Suddenly the app I was so excited about seems… silly. Small. But I know it's not and it's only my nerves trying to trip me up.

"I've found a start-up working on something interesting." I pass out copies of their prospectus to everyone. I know people prefer digital copies here, but I like the more immediate physicality of paper. It makes things more real. "They want to be a one-stop shop for women's health. A menstruation tracker, a mood tracker, automatic reminders for important doctor's appointments, a symptoms tracker, suggested meditation tracks, workout guides, journaling prompts, and self-care tips. Basically everything a woman needs for a healthy body and mind."

Finn flips through the packet I've handed him. "Why just women? Men need to be healthy too."

"Because women take on most of the burden of the health-care needs for the men and children in their lives. And no one does it in return for them."

They all shift guiltily, probably remembering all the times their wives and girlfriends nagged them about going to the doctor.

"The user interface looks good," Logan says.

I nod. "I'd say it's one of the best things they have going for them. And the test app I tried this weekend was remarkably bug-free."

"Their projected user-base growth is pretty rapid. Probably too rapid." Finn is clearly skeptical.

"It is," I admit. I had my own concerns about that. "But they're ambitious. They want to go big."

"How are they going to make money?" Mark asks. "Selling this information to advertisers is… tricky."

"No ads," I say. "Nothing gets sold. The data is all encrypted, completely secure. It'll be a subscription model in terms of revenue."

"That's a tough sell," Mark says. "People want their apps to be free."

"I believe they'll pay when it's worth it. If you look at the initial growth of the user base, it's very impressive. And they have an innovative marketing plan to reach even more customers."

"They're keeping their operations lean," Logan says. "I like it. Do you think they know what they're talking about when it comes to the marketing?"

"Their market is women with smartphones, which is a pretty big target audience. And let's face it—most apps are designed with men in mind. Women can use them too, but the ideal end user is almost always a man."

"What percentage of their team are women?" Finn asks.

I grin at him. Trust Finn to get at the smart questions. "Ninety. They've got one guy working on the back end of the programming and that's it."

Dev closes the information packet with a decisive snap of his wrist. "I like it."

Mark focuses on him, something dark in his gaze. "You didn't even ask any questions."

Logan turns to face Dev, then Finn too. They're waiting for Dev to respond to Mark's… question? Challenge?

Normally I'd defuse the situation, not that they ever *really* fought before, not beyond brotherly bickering. Dev's acquisition of Corvus has changed that, made the barbed comments attain spikes that can truly cut.

It's not my job to manage them anymore. If they want to fight, I have to stand back and let them.

"Do you have any questions?" I fold my hands. "Because I'd like to offer them funding soon."

"I trust you," Dev says.

The word *trust* has Finn's mouth flattening to meanness. And Finn is never mean.

"Great." Logan snaps down the word like a prospectus he's rejecting. "I don't have anything else for today."

"Me either," Finn adds.

A look passes between him, Logan, and Mark. Like they've decided on something.

Dev doesn't notice. He's back to his laptop. It doesn't look like he's going to add to the meeting at all.

"Are we going to discuss the Corvus breakup, or are you

going to do that all on your own too?" The edge to Mark's voice isn't at all hidden.

Logan crosses his arms while Finn sets one elbow on the table to lean in. All three of them are bristling at Dev.

"I'm currently going through the archives." Dev doesn't even blink. "Assets will start being catalogued for future sale next week."

Which isn't a discussion in the slightest, just Dev telling them what he's going to do.

I set my palms on the table. "Are you firing all the employees? What about the contracts Corvus already had in place? And the programs they developed? That needs to be hashed out."

Dev glances at me, then away. "I'm not ready to discuss that."

Finn falls back in his chair, shaking his head. "Whatever, dude. You do whatever the fuck you want with all of it." He stabs a finger into the table. "Except the panopticon stuff. Doc gets that."

Dev says nothing.

"He's right," Logan says. "And Callie's entitled to the *Tidbytes* archives."

"January and Grace will want to look at the spyware stuff," Mark says.

Elliot isn't here to say what Minerva deserves, but maybe she already stole everything she wanted from Corvus and has it sitting on her infamous hard drive.

Dev looks at me. This time he doesn't look away. His gaze is precise, almost deft. "Do you have any demands? Since we're making a list."

Finn erupts out of his chair. "Oh fuck you. *Fuck* you. I don't know what's going on with you, what's in that head of yours, but we came up *together*. You remember that, that stuffy, shitty garage? It was all of us working on that program, not just Mr. Math Genius. And when we started

32

this firm, it was all of us building it. Again, not just Mr. Math Genius. But only you get to get inside Corvus when it's finally down?"

He storms out without waiting for an answer.

Logan sighs and tosses his pen on the table. The heavy fountain pen clatters like a gong. "Well, that went awesome. Just peachy."

Mark rubs his forehead. When he speaks, it's soft and to Dev. "I don't know what it is with you and this takeover. If it's something personal, fine. But we've all got personal scores to settle with Corvus, and we haven't kept them secret from each other." His hand falls and he pins Dev with a stare. "Just something to consider before you drive everybody away."

He and Logan walk out together. Leaving me, Dev, and a shocked Yancy.

"Not a word," I say to her. She shuts her mouth. "If even a whisper of this leaves this room, I will know. And you will be fired with extreme prejudice."

Her face goes bone white. But she nods.

I probably shouldn't have scared her so much, but this... this was bad. No one needs to know how bad. Or that the Bastards might be close to breaking up.

My heart trembles at the thought. They were always so united, together in everything. Yes, they disagreed and argued and were rough-and-tumble with each other, but this is something different.

This feels broken.

Dev steeples his fingers, his expression thoughtful. I want to yell at him, shake him, somehow impress on him how awful that was. How upset he should be by it.

"You didn't ask for anything," he says.

I open my mouth, shut it again. "What would I ever want from Corvus?"

He glances at Yancy.

33

I shake my head. "You can tell her to leave. It doesn't have to be mediated through me now. I'm a partner."

His expression goes blank. "Of course. I'm sorry."

Yancy's already grabbing her stuff and heading for the door. "I'll just... just..." She's gone before she can think up even a halfway-decent excuse.

Dev is very still, very expressionless. Inscrutable.

I want to fix this. To bring them all back together and force them to hug, to apologize, to bring Dev back into the fold. But... but I'm beginning to think Dev's not capable of that.

And it's not my job anymore.

"I don't want anything from Corvus," I say to his earlier question. I gather up my stuff, intending to go after Yancy, explain things. Gently. I point to the door that the other Bastards went through, away from Dev. "But they do."

He doesn't say another word as I leave.

CHAPTER 5

I blow out a long breath and pat down my skirt before I knock on Dev's office door. *This is just a meeting between partners. Happens all the time here at Bastard Capital.*

It's been a week since my first meeting as a partner, and I'm starting to find my way in this new role. Yancy has the office-manager stuff handled—I've got no worries there—and my focus has been entirely on finding companies to fund. The founders I've talked to are all very excited to meet with me.

I'm starting to feel completely like a partner now. So this meeting ought to be no big deal. Except this is Dev. He's not just another partner here, no matter how hard I pretend. And he wanted to meet with me alone. On a private matter.

I can't imagine what it is. He's not going to bring up our relationship or lack of it—he's not the type. When I told him no, he heard me and he respects that.

I might have been obsessing over what could have been in the still of the night as I tried to fall asleep, but that's my problem. Dev's given no sign that he's taken my rejection personally. Or anything else personally.

So what might be the personal thing Dev wants to meet with me about?

I lift my fist and knock. Firm, quick.

"Come in." Even through the door, his deep voice tickles my sensitive places.

I set my shoulders and walk in.

His office isn't as impersonal as Elliot's was. That's because he had me decorate it. I chose grays and blues that look as if they were once deep but have been faded by time and the sun. The sofa is simple but still comfortable, the coffee table made of polished driftwood, his desk done in darkest cherry. The art is abstract, black-and-white photos of desert landscapes. Not dunes, but the rocky, scrubby deserts of Southern California, with Joshua trees and saguaro cacti breaking up the endless dryness.

I chose stark yet organic lines for his office. If I were doing it over again today, I'd choose something even bleaker. No driftwood, no landscapes. Just pure abstraction.

He takes one of the chairs by the sofa, gesturing for me to join him. "Thank you for coming."

I arrange my skirt as I sit down. It's a thirties style with a tight bodice and a skirt that skims my hips and thighs. No crinoline or full skirts to wrestle with, but the skirt still needs some styling when I sit.

I set my crossed hands on my knees. "What did you need?"

My heart is pounding, but there's no way he can tell.

"I need... I need discretion." He leans toward me, his gaze intent. "You're the only one I can trust with this."

Trust. I almost choke on the word. "Dev, all those things I said—"

"Please." His tone is strained. "Don't say no yet. I need you."

Of all the things he could have said, that's even worse than *trust.* I want him to be happy. I want his dreams to come true.

And I want to make it happen for him. But he has to come

at least halfway to meet happiness. Which he doesn't even seem close to doing.

I grip my knee, flick my gaze to the ceiling. "What is it?"

Hearing him out won't cost me anything. And I can still say no.

I hear him shift, draw a deep breath. I won't let myself look though. "What I'm going to say, no one else knows. And I'd appreciate it if it didn't get around."

I snap my gaze to him. "I thought you trusted me."

He lifts his palms. "I do. It's just very sensitive."

I wet my lips. "Go on. You know I won't say a word."

"I never talk about my family."

The entire world knows about that. Dev, the mysterious one, the founder who came out of nowhere. The one who wrote the core algorithm that made them all rich.

I know that about him. And that he went to Cal State Fullerton. And that he's very sensitive to earworms.

A tiny, pitiful collection of facts. I don't linger on what I know about his kissing ability or how I feel about him. That way lies madness.

"Do you want to talk about them?" Reconciling with family even when it hurts—I know all about that. I wouldn't say I'm good at it, but I'm trying.

I can help him with it too.

A small, wry smile plays at his lips. "I would if I knew who they were. I grew up in the Sacramento Children's Home."

A noise escapes me. Tiny, wounded. "You… Your parents left you? What happened?"

I've had my problems with my family—God knows that— but I'd never wish them away. They hurt me, badly, but they also loved me. It's why I never really gave up on my dream of having a family of my own.

Dev probably never had that particular dream. And I'm beginning to understand why.

"I was left at a fire station when I was a newborn. As best as they could tell, my mother took me there when I was only a few hours old."

He's telling all this in a low monotone, as if it's someone else's life. Actually, I think he'd put more emotion into someone else's story. I put my hand over my mouth, the better to hold in my grief. What an awful beginning. My heart is breaking for him.

I don't know that it provides an excuse for why he is how he is, but it's a damn good explanation. A wrenching one.

"My name is just Dev. Short for nothing. The station was on Devon Street, which they shortened to Dev. And my last name is a mash-up of the last names of the two firefighters who found me."

"There…" I swallow down some tears. "Your mother didn't leave a note? Or anything?"

He's dry-eyed. "No. I had a blanket, and a dish towel repurposed as a diaper. That's all."

"Didn't the police look for her?" I can't imagine someone just leaving him and never looking back. Especially his own mother.

"They never found anything." His expression is masklike. "I doubt they looked very hard."

"You've never told anyone this?" I'm baffled by his lack of emotion. How can he tell this story—for the very first time—and just… not react? At all?

"No. It wasn't important."

I'd call it absolutely important. It explains so much about his mysterious past, his lack of a family, and his trust issues. No wonder he doesn't see that the Bastards are his family. He's never had one.

But he could see that if he'd only give a little and open up to them. They'd understand completely if he told them all this. What's broken between them could be repaired.

"How did you end up in a group home?" I ask that through my spread fingers.

He shrugs. "There were some foster families. A lot. I don't think I spent more than a few months in any one place, but I haven't seen my records, so I can't confirm."

"Your records?" That makes him sound like an inmate.

"I was a ward of the state. I've got a paper trail from here to the moon. But I can't see it."

So even that small bit of his past is denied him. "Maybe Elliot could—"

"He can't."

I don't bother to ask if he's even talked to Elliot about the possibility.

Dev stares off at the atrium. "Anyway, there were some foster homes, but eventually I ended up in the group home. And stayed. It… I didn't mind it."

Like he got bumped on a flight or something and nothing more.

Inside, I'm shaking like a leaf. This is a terrible, awful story, and the fact that he's so closed off from it, his own flipping story, makes it that much worse. But I hold myself still, my voice steady. "I'm very sorry that happened to you." I catch myself right before my voice breaks. "And I'm glad that you trusted me enough to tell me. But… I don't understand how I can help you."

He shifts, suddenly fidgety. Upset. "There might be a chance that my parents' identity is out there. In some government record."

I sit up. "How? Where could it be?"

Again he shifts. "Fuchs came to me a few years ago. Right when we started Bastard Capital."

Oh no. If Fuchs is entering the story, it can't be good. He used to run Corvus before Dev bought it and forced him out. Fuchs has brought nothing but awfulness to everyone he touches.

"What did he want?"

"He knew I'd developed the core algorithm. He wanted me to come work for him at Corvus."

Chills run over my skin. It sounds so simple, but nothing involving Fuchs ever is. "What did he offer you?"

I think I already know, but if Dev never spoke of his past before, how could that be?

"He knew everything about my childhood," Dev says. Not shocked, not surprised. "He had my records, although he wouldn't show me."

My fists clench. What a horrible, horrible asshole. If Fuchs were here now, I'd risk my manicure and slap the crap out of him.

"He said that he had government records no one else had. Things that agencies had forgotten they even had."

"Oh, Dev. He was lying."

His gaze locks with mine. This time it's a hammer. "But what if he wasn't? He told me he'd found my parents' identities. That I could have them if I went to work for Corvus."

I gasp. I knew that was coming, but the breath is still knocked out of me. "He didn't. He couldn't. You know that."

Dev shakes his head. "He had my records. And Corvus had all these government contracts. They got access to all kinds of records. They could have found my parents."

I twist my hands together to keep from reaching for him. "That doesn't mean he found those particular records even if they exist. You told him no, so you must understand that."

His eyes—bright, feverish—tells me that he doesn't. "I wasn't going to work for him. But if I could access Corvus's records another way..."

I fall back into the sofa. The enormity of it is baffling. "You... you bought Corvus just to get those particular records? Which they might not even have?"

It must have cost him billions to get the shares in Corvus he needed. And who knows what favors he promised to the board members for their votes against Fuchs. And while I'm not sad Corvus is being dismantled, there are a lot of people who are going to lose their jobs there.

"My parents are in the archives somewhere," he says. "And I'm going to find them."

"All right." I take a breath, then another. "All right. Say that it's in the archive. And you find it. And then you find your parents. And then what?"

He blinks at me like there is no *then what.*

I understand wanting to know his parents. I want him to know his parents, to find some closure or knowledge or something, but family isn't magical. It can't heal everything in you. Sometimes it only makes things worse.

"Well, then I'll know," he says. "Who they are, what they're like." The spark of hope in his voice is young, boyish.

I want this for him, so badly, but… but I'm also terrified for him. He can't be open and honest with the people already in his life who love him. What's going to happen when he meets the people who abandoned him when he was only hours old? Who never came back for him?

I can't help but worry it's going to be a disaster. But there's no way I'd stop him even if I could.

"I hope the information is there," I say. "But you don't need my help with the archives. Tell Finn or Logan or even Mark." I smile, thinking how this would help heal the rift between them all. If they heard this, they'd understand Dev better. "They're the perfect people for this."

"Oh no, I don't need your help accessing the archives." He frowns like that's ridiculous. "That's not what I asked you here for."

"Then what?"

"I need your help to find Fuchs."

CHAPTER 6

I made her cry.

She tried to hold it in, but when I was telling her about my childhood, I saw the tears. They nestled in the corners of her eyes, diamond drops of sadness.

I didn't cry. My heart was wild, banging through my chest as I told her, but I held everything else back. There's no point crying. It doesn't change the story, and I can't tell it if I'm weeping.

Besides, I'm a successful man now. My past has no bearing on who I am. I've transcended it, escaped my predetermined fate. No one can pity me.

I don't want their pity. I hate it.

Anjelica's moved past the pity now that I've asked her to find Fuchs. She's sailed right into anger.

"No. You're crazy. He's gone and let him stay gone." She's up off the couch, her chest rising and falling with her rapid breaths. The color in her cheeks is high and bright. She's inexpressibly beautiful.

"I would ask Minerva for help," I say, "but I can't trust her. Fuchs knows exactly where the files are, how to unlock them. It has to be him."

I've thought long and hard about it as I went through the

archives. Hours and hours spent searching and thinking. This is the quickest, most certain way to find them.

"Emily," Anjelica corrects absently. "Her real name is Emily."

"Yes, well, I still can't trust her."

Anjelica's mouth purses. She doesn't much trust Minerva/Emily herself. "I still think anyone else would be better at this. Paul." She shakes a finger at me. "He knows everyone. And he could find Fuchs so much faster."

"Why don't you want to help me?" I ask quietly. "Is it because of what's between us?"

She told me no, and I won't cross that line. I've never crossed that line. I dream of her, I shake inside with how much I want her, need to be near her... but I don't show it. If she doesn't believe that I can hold to that line, that's probably why she's protesting.

"I respect what you said before," I say when she doesn't answer. "The kiss... I misunderstood. I won't again."

At least not until I've found what I need in the Corvus archives. Once I've put together the puzzle of my past, I can try again with her. I'll have to prove to her that I'm worthy of her, that she can take that chance with me, but I'll do it.

If I don't... Well, I just won't let myself fail.

"That's not why." Her answer is as quiet as my question. "I just don't think I can. The others... they should know this."

"I can't tell them why I really took over Corvus. We're already close to splitting up the firm."

If they cast me out, I'll be completely alone. I'm used to it, but I don't want that. I can fix the rift as it is now. If it widens, our friendship will be done for.

"You can tell them anything," Anjelica says.

She can tell them anything. They love her, probably more than they love each other and only slightly less than they love their wives. Anjelica is our glue, always has been. Without her, Bastard Capital would have dissolved under the weight of our differing personalities in the first few months.

"I'm not telling them," I say. "But I told you and now I need your help. You understand people. You know what they want."

"Not Fuchs. No one knows what he wants except for maybe Minerva. He's not even human it seems. You—" She snaps her mouth shut tight, guilt staining her cheeks.

"I'm not human either, so I'd understand him?" I suggest quietly. I know she doesn't actually believe that, so I won't allow her words to wound me.

"That's not what I meant. You run in the same circles. You've actually spoken to him. You know the people who might have had contact with him." She crosses her arms as if she's scored a major point.

I shake my head. "I've talked to them—no one's seen or heard from him. His houses are empty, his phones are dead, and he's gone off the grid. I don't even know where to start."

"Why not start at the beginning?" She bites her lip like she wishes she could take that back.

"The beginning?"

"Where he's from. Where his family still is."

"Opole, Poland," I say without thinking.

She raises her eyebrows. "You know that?"

"I've memorized a lot about him."

I know where he was born, the date of his birth, when his family came to the States—I even have his elementary school report cards. But I need Anjelica to help me assemble these facts into a search pattern. She understands people in a way I can't. Algorithms are easy. People are impossible.

Except for Anjelica. She's one of the few people I want to take the trouble to understand.

"I always thought he was German," Anjelica says.

"He is. There are still some ethnic Germans in Poland.

But the family came here when he was only eight. To Chicago."

She lifts her palm. "There you go. Two places to start looking."

This is a dismissal. She's going to pass this off as "helping" me.

I'm not going to let her. I need more. I need Fuchs, and I need to find my parents. She's given the other Bastards their heart's desire—why can't I have mine? Why do only I get half measures from her?

"You asked me what I want." I harden my tone. She has to understand how serious I am. "Well, I want this. Will you help me or not?"

She exhales through her nose, slow and resigned. "If this is really what you want, then yes. But I have a condition too."

She doesn't give anyone else conditions when they ask for her help. Just me. But I nod anyway.

"You don't know what I'm going to ask for," she warns.

"It doesn't matter. I'll give you whatever you want."

I mean that as deeply as I've ever meant anything. From the moment I first saw her, all she had to do was ask, and I'd make it hers. Things she didn't even ask for too—raises, a bigger office... and my heart.

Her mouth tenses. "If we find out about your parents, you have to tell the others about this. Maybe not all of it, but the important parts."

She's so sure that if I pour my heart out to the guys, everything will be forgiven. That I'll suddenly have the same kind of relationship she does with them.

I'm not convinced, but once I find my parents, it won't matter. I'll be able to tell them whatever Anjelica wants because then I'll finally have a story of my own.

And when I do that, give her what she wants, things will change between us. I can already see it.

"Sure." I hold out my hand. "You've got a deal."

She lifts her hand, then hesitates. The way her fingers curl, half toward me, half toward her, reminds me of a bridge, one connecting across the space between us.

But it's not a bridge, because she doesn't want to touch me.

I let my hand drop, flex my fingers. "Or not a deal. There're no binding terms or anything."

Her mouth purses. "No." She shoves her hand at me. "When you find your parents, you tell them everything. That is binding."

This time *I* hesitate. "But what do you want?"

She wants me to make amends with the Bastards, to fix everything between me and them… but that's not specifically for *her*.

"That's what I want." Her eyes are screwed up in confusion like she really doesn't understand.

I take her hand, pull her closer. Her eyes widen, but she comes.

"No." I'm rock firm, because she's not wriggling out of this. "You. You personally. That's what you want for them. I'm talking about you."

She so rarely asks for things for herself. She'll give others everything but won't take a crumb for herself. It's a damn crime in my opinion.

We're so close I can see the flutter of her eyelashes, the tiny quiver at the corner of her eye, the flare of her nose with each inhale. She's beautiful, so beautiful, but these small, private bits of animation in her features make her radiant.

"That's all I want," she says. "Nothing else."

I can't tell if she's lying or if that's what she really believes. Anjelica always focuses on others, on their wants, their dreams, but what about hers? Is becoming partner all she ever wanted? Is her life complete now?

I can't ask her that. And now that she's told me that she wants nothing else, I have to respect that.

I let go of her hand. "Fine. If we find my parents, I tell everyone everything."

She doesn't step away as quickly as I expected. "Good. It's agreed."

Our eyes lock and—

I shake my head, step back. We have to stop doing that. I can't believe in the things I see in her eyes. She already said it wasn't going to work.

CHAPTER 7

We fly into Kraków and stay the first night there. The city is charming, beautiful, and filled with the kind of antiquities you just don't see in America. History is right in front of you, always in a place like this. There are main squares and public markets and massive monuments and old churches and even a castle. It's all too delicious.

Everyone is friendly too, although I get a lot of stares, way more than I get at home. I guess retro really isn't a thing in Europe.

Dev rents a car, driving confidently through the streets, shifting like he does it every day. We've talked very little during the flight, the both of us working on our laptops. But there's nothing to distract me now from his sheer physical presence. He moves... he moves like no one I've ever seen. Elegant, but precise. No gesture wasted. It makes his every motion all that much more potent.

"I don't think I would've been brave enough to drive."

The look he sends me is quick, to the point. "You would have." He brakes when a truck swings out in front of us, downshifting without looking. "You *can* drive a stick?"

Memories flood me, of the engine stalling out yet again,

Kaleb's gentle, encouraging smile. He never got angry, not once. I was the angry one.

I pinch my lips together. "Nope. Never had to learn. Where'd you learn?"

His brow furrows. He looks for a moment like he won't answer. "I needed a way to get to campus in college. All I could afford was an old beat-up stick shift. So I taught myself in a parking lot."

I can see him doing it too, forcing himself over and over to get it right, to try again, wearing that exact same furrowed brow. "How many clutches did you burn out?"

His mouth twitches. "Two. So I had to learn how to replace those."

Something I've never forgotten about him is that he used to work in an auto-parts factory. I think I might be the only person in his life who knows that. "Did you make the clutches yourself? When you worked in the parts factory?"

Surprise splashes over his face, like he never thought I'd remember. "No, they made specialty parts. Not clutches for old beaters."

"Oh." I want to ask him if he's fabricated anything recently—he told me he used to like to make things in machine shops, at the same time he told me about the factory job. But that would be too personal.

Personal is dangerous with us.

He upshifts, passing a slow, hulking van. I can't seem to look away from how his hand curls over the shifter knob.

"I lied," I say suddenly. "I do know how to drive stick. Or at least I learned once."

Immediately I regret it, turning to face the window. I don't want to talk about Kaleb, not with anyone, but especially not with Dev. Except my lie was sitting like a rock in my stomach.

I wait for him to press further, to ask who taught me, when I learned, why I lied.

But I forgot that's not how Dev operates.

"Do you want to drive then?" he asks, completely serious.

I laugh. It bursts out of me, popping open my mouth. "No, I don't. When I said learned, I definitely meant past tense."

There's something like a smile pulling at his mouth, but not quite, and then the tension between us recedes a bit, lets us both breathe. And enjoy the views of the city.

We pull up in front of a gorgeous castle, or at least something designed to look like a castle. But it's more on the Brothers Grimm end of the fairy-tale spectrum than the Disney one. I immediately love it.

"This is a hotel?" I ask as we walk inside.

"I didn't make reservations," he says as he hauls our luggage into the lobby. "But they should have something."

"You're not going to pull the old 'only one room left in the hotel' trick?"

He stiffens. "I'd never do that to you." He sounds offended. Shocked.

"I was only joking," I say softly. I realize suddenly that I don't joke with him. Everyone else, yes. But when he and I decided we'd never act on our attraction while we were working together, easy friendliness went right out the window. Things were too brittle between us for anything but strictest professionalism. "I know you wouldn't."

He ducks his head, his mouth tightening. "I don't— Sometimes I don't know how to act around you. I want you and you said no. I need..." He draws in a long breath through his nose. "I would never disrespect your wishes."

He's never this vulnerable. Not ever. He's either inscrutable or something close to it.

I suck in a breath, my heart stuttering. Never being vulnerable might be his way of hiding his uncertainty. To disguise that he doesn't know how to act sometimes. I can't let him see my reaction because he'll mistake it for pity.

But he does make jokes. I've seen him do it with the other guys. So he understands humor.

"Sorry, I shouldn't have made light about the hotel situation," I say. "I wasn't thinking."

Why did I never realize his cool blankness might be a cover for something else? Probably because I was too busy trying not to look at him at all.

Someone official-looking comes up to Dev then. "Mr. Arman, so glad to see you again! It's always a pleasure when you stay with us."

I cut a glance at Dev. So this isn't his first time here. And why would he have been here before?

"Poland is the Silicon Valley of Europe," he explains. "A start-up I invested in has a team here. I come to check on things occasionally."

I know the part about Poland's tech industry but not about his start-up. Or his numerous trips here. Which is a silly thing to keep from me—why hide a business trip? Is the secrecy unthinking on his part or purposeful?

"Your usual suite?" The manager discreetly clears his throat. "Or will you need two suites?"

"Two suites." I hold out my hand, cutting through the awkwardness. "I'm the newest partner at Bastard Capital. Anjelica Caprice."

He shakes my hand with more enthusiasm than finesse. "Ah, how lovely." The way he runs his gaze up and down my body says he finds me personally lovely too. "We hope you enjoy your stay."

The manager is still holding my hand when Dev says without inflection, "Give her my usual suite. I'll take the other one." His face is made of stone and is just as unmovable.

He's jealous. The thought hits me with a pulse of delight. I smoosh it under the thumb of my better sense. It doesn't matter if he's jealous, because we're business partners only.

In fact, it's better if he isn't.

"Excellent." The manager releases me and claps his hands together. Instantly several uniformed employees are taking the bags, ushering us toward the elevators.

I'm impressed, even after all the luxury hotels I've stayed in on Bastard business. Dev, however, looks as if he'd be happy never speaking again.

The porters show us to our rooms, mine right next door to Dev's. The suite is on the smaller side but amazingly charming. There's a sitting room, an attached bedroom with a canopy bed, and a fantastic bathroom with a marble tub I could do laps in. Maybe I will later.

I go to the windows and look out on the square beneath us. There's a patch of green, some vendors selling food, and plenty of people visiting and chatting. No one seems in too much of a hurry, which is such a nice change from the City.

I'm not sure what the plan is for tonight. We're not supposed to go to Opole until tomorrow, so I've got a few hours to kill. And some jet lag to sleep off.

And a tub worthy of a princess waiting in the bathroom.

As I head for it, my phone buzzes on the coffee table. The notifications tell me that Dev has texted me.

Did that manager bother you?

I roll my eyes. He might have asked me that to my face. And besides, I didn't reach the ripe old age of twenty-seven without figuring out how to handle overeager guys. Or at least endure them.

It was fine. He was harmless. Really, eyeballing me while he drew out the word *lovely* was even less than harmless. I've heard much worse.

It didn't seem that way.
If you were so bothered, why didn't you say something then?
I didn't want to embarrass you.
If I'd felt unsafe, you would have known.
Safe is the bare minimum here. That's…

I wait, but nothing more comes. Not a correction, an addition, nothing.

This might be another one of those moments where he doesn't know how to act with me.

I set my phone aside and try the connecting door. It opens easily and right into his room, no second door there.

He blinks at me, his phone still in his hand. He's got his concentrating face on, like he's trying to translate what he wants to say. Well, he can say it to my face. We're both adults.

"I was fine," I say. "I appreciate your concern, but all he did was stare at me for a little too long and shake my hand for a little too long. If he does it again, you can flatten him then."

"I don't flatten people."

But he could. Those lean muscles don't fool me.

"No, you get Finn to do it for you."

He raises an eyebrow. "And you don't?"

My face falls. "You know about that?"

"Fuck." He tosses his phone down. "I shouldn't have said anything. Finn, he needed some help with hacking into the banking stuff."

My knees go wobbly. "The… the banking stuff? Finn never said anything about banking stuff."

Dev pulls out a chair for me. "He deserved everything we did to him."

I sink down into it. About two years ago, this guy I dated once—*once*—decided he was going to stalk me. On the web, in real life, everywhere. I got emails, DMs, posts on my Facebook profile, even good old-fashioned snail mail. All begging me to give him one more chance. And threatening to kill himself if I didn't.

I ignored it for a week. And then he hacked my email.

So I called in Finn to see if he could help. Finn never told me exactly what he did, but I got shiny new accounts for everything, a PO box, and better security at my house. And I never heard from the guy again.

"What *did* you do to him?"

Dev's mouth flattens. "I don't know that Finn would appreciate my telling you. But he's never coming back."

I lift my hands. "Okay, if this involves concrete shoes or unmarked desert graves, I changed my mind. I don't want to know."

Dev snorts. "Give us some credit. We're much more elegant than that."

Elegant. Yes, he is. Not Finn, but definitely Dev.

He catches me staring at him. "It wasn't that bad," he says. "I promise he's still alive."

"I believe you," I say. "It's just… I never knew you helped Finn with that."

He looks away. "We would do anything for you. You know that."

That's not what I meant. I meant him personally, not the rest of them. But he clearly doesn't want to take any credit.

"Sorry." I get up, inch toward the door. "I shouldn't have barged in."

"I left it unlocked."

Which means what? I can't see his face, and there's nothing in his voice to read. It's like trying to put emotions and motivations onto a blank page.

Except he went after that guy for me. Did something so bad to him that Dev won't tell me. His face might be blank, but his actions aren't.

"Still, I shouldn't have." I slip through the doorway, safe on my side of the rooms. "I'll just lock it then."

He doesn't stop me.

CHAPTER 8

I don't know what the hell I was thinking, strong-arming Anjelica into helping me, but it's a fucking disaster so far.

Not her personally. She's amazing and beautiful and making friends everywhere we go even though she doesn't speak any Polish. She's happily posed for a ton of pictures—I guess no one's ever seen someone who dresses like she does —and traded Instagram handles and tasted sausage and beer and rye bread and stuffed cabbage leaves. All with a wide smile and an open heart.

I envy how happy she is with others, with the entire world.

No, the problem isn't her—it's me. She's easy with everyone, and I'm completely uneasy with her. I can't stop thinking of her lips, her laugh, the way my palms ache to touch her. I'm out in the freezing cold, and she's the only source of warmth… and I can't get any closer.

We're driving to Opole, me in the driver's seat, her next to me, and she's exclaiming over each interesting thing she sees. We've already stopped three times so she could get out and explore.

I don't mind except that it's prolonging how long I have

to be in such close contact with her. The cold wouldn't hurt so bad if I wasn't constantly reminded of how hot she is.

"It's hard to believe Fuchs was born here."

"Hmm?" I can see her knee out of the corner of my eye, clad in some kind of silky stocking, and it's fucking with my focus. Real bad.

Those knees shift, part, and I have to clutch the stick shift hard to keep from driving us off the road.

"This place is so nice," she says. "The landscape, the food, the people… I can't see Fuchs here."

"I don't think it was so nice under the Soviets," I say. "Or the Nazis. Or whoever invaded before that."

"Good point." She frowns at the windshield.

"Maybe that's why he never came back," I say. "He didn't feel like he belonged."

I know the feeling, although there's no sense of belonging to be found in a children's home. At least in the foster homes there might have been a chance of pretending that it was real, that it could be your own family if you squinted hard. But in the barracks-like dorms, the dining hall, nothing to call your own…

She's looking at me like she knows what I'm thinking about. Which maybe she does—she can read people like no one I've ever met.

"Maybe we won't find anything here then."

The disappointment in her voice stings me.

"We won't know unless we check. And maybe he's here because he figures no one will think to look."

"Or maybe he's in a yurt in Mongolia."

I try to imagine checking every single yurt on the steppes, yelling Arne Fuchs's name into countless tent flaps. Riding day and night on the tough little Mongolian ponies. The endless sky above us, the one the Mongolians worshipped in Genghis Khan's time.

"I was joking," she says when I don't speak. "We shouldn't go to Mongolia."

"Because he's not there or because you don't want to?"

"Have you ever been?" She's leaning toward me, her breasts straining against her dress. She never wears anything low cut—probably because that would reveal her tattoos—but her breasts are distracting enough without the hints of skin. It's the cut of the bodice, the tucks hugging the swells of her breasts, just like my hands want to.

"Um." My hands tighten on the wheel. What the fuck was she asking? I make my expression still, my breathing even. "No. Not yet."

"So you want to?"

We talked like this before, when we first met and all we did was walk together. Once she started working for us, it had to stop.

I wonder if I'd have told her about my past much sooner if we kept on with those walks. If I'd have spilled everything without being forced. I can't say. I've never told anyone before.

But with her I was tempted immediately.

"Yeah," I say. "It seems like it'd be a great adventure. The kind you can't find most places."

"This is an adventure too," she says breezily.

I cut a glance at her. "We're looking for Arne Fuchs, the worst asshole in probably ever. When we find him, it won't be pleasant. He might have tried to kill Minerva, remember?"

A chill races over my ribs, pricking each bone. Maybe I should have left her behind. If Fuchs tries something and she's hurt...

"Did they ever figure out if it was him?" The dreamy quality is gone from her voice.

"He didn't say when he talked to Minerva the last time. And then he disappeared before she could ask him."

Her lips purse, a tiny frown appearing between her brows. "Should we be calling her Emily? Elliot does."

I'm about to say that I don't care what Elliot calls her—she's not my girlfriend—and that Minerva suits her better, but I hold back. That would give too much away about how I feel about Minerva. How I don't trust her and never will.

And then my pause stretches into a new, different realization. I can't say that to Anjelica because it would hurt her. She wants me to fix my relationship with the other guys, not slag on their girlfriends. Even the girlfriends she's not sure about herself.

"Maybe we should call her Emily around Elliot."

I watch her reaction carefully from the corner of my eye, trying to see if I got it right. My instinct would be to not call her anything in front of Elliot, to avoid talking about her at all, but that's not what Anjelica wants to hear.

She mulls over that. "That's probably the best thing. Although I think Elliot really loves her."

My thoughts go to white noise. I don't know if Elliot is in love, and I don't want to know. It's just too much, all of them pairing off.

When Logan got married, it was fine. I was happy for him. It didn't affect his work, which made me happy for the firm. And then they separated and he fell apart.

It scared the shit out of me. He just… hollowed out. He looked on the outside how I feel on the inside. I couldn't imagine risking that kind of pain for any woman. Except Anjelica.

But then it got even worse, because they *all* started to pair off. They were happy, in love, always smiling, and I felt like even more of an outsider. Anjelica helped their relationships too. She was their fairy godmother, sprinkling her magic over their happily-ever-after.

She never did that for me.

"What do you think?" Her gaze is clear.

I think I shouldn't have any opinion at all about Elliot's love life. "He risked a lot for her" is what I finally come up with.

It's an understatement since they still can't enter the country, Minerva is wanted by the FBI, and Elliot's looking at disbarment along with several other federal crimes. They're working things out with the government, but it could be months or years before everything's untangled.

"I never would have expected that from Elliot," she says. "So he must be in love."

I'm saved by the arrival of Opole on the horizon. Anjelica leans forward and exclaims when she sees it.

"It's just as cute as Kraków," she says, "except smaller."

I don't know if I'd call it cute, but nothing much ever strikes me as cute. When we cross the river into the city, she looks out over it like a kid seeing Santa on Christmas. Jesus, how does she just *enjoy* everything so much?

We're supposed to meet my contact at a coffee shop near the university. Luckily no one stops us for a picture with Anjelica as we park the car and walk to meet her. She's already waiting for us inside.

I don't bother to order. I take the seat next to my contact, ready to get down to business. Anjelica looks longingly at the menu on the wall—she usually drinks coffee throughout the day—but we can grab a coffee after, when we're on the way back to Kraków.

"What did you find?" I ask.

My contact, a twentysomething hacker with light brown hair and piercingly dark eyes, raises an eyebrow. "Nothing. I even ran the search algorithm you sent twice. If he's here, the cameras haven't caught him."

She pushes her laptop across to me so I can see what she's done.

"Cameras?" Anjelica asks. "And am I allowed to introduce myself?"

"Anjelica, Zuzanna. Zuzanna, Anjelica." I start to scroll through the data Zuzanna's pulled off the camera network in the city. "As for the cameras, all of the EU is wired up. There's no place left to hide here."

"Ah." Anjelica isn't stupid—she immediately understands that I've hired Zuzanna to break into the camera network and search for any pictures of Fuchs from the past few weeks. I wrote the facial recognition program she used myself, so I know it's pretty damn good.

It's also found nothing.

I tweak some parameters, set it to run again. I don't ask permission, because Zuzanna knows I pay well enough that she can let me do whatever I want with her laptop.

When I look up again, they're gone.

My heart does this sort of nauseating lurch. Anjelica can't be lost. How will I find her again?

When I see her in the line with Zuzanna, my lungs fill with cool air. The two of them have their heads together like old friends, and Zuzanna points to the menu like she's explaining it to Anjelica. They come back with coffees and at least three plates of pastries.

We haven't even had lunch and Anjelica's already on dessert.

She sets a mug of coffee in front of me. "So you can keep up your strength."

I stare at it and the plates of sweets. My program is going to finish running in a few seconds, but Anjelica's not going to be done by then.

She offers me something that looks like a donut. *"Pączki?"*

Zuzanna giggles at her pronunciation.

"We're almost done here." I frown.

Anjelica takes a bite and moans in appreciation. "You sure you don't want one?"

There's a tiny bit of melted sugar at the corner of her

mouth. My own tongue reaches out, touches the exact corner of my own lips. But there's no sugar there.

When I do that, Anjelica covers her mouth. "Sorry." When her hand drops, the sugar is gone.

I missed her licking it off. Fuck.

"Do you want me to pull more images off the camera network?"

Zuzanna's question drags me out of my idiotic thoughts. "No." Her laptop chimes, telling me my program is finished. And there're no hits. I sigh and push it back toward Zuzanna. "He's not here. Thank you though. Usual payment method?"

Zuzanna nods as Anjelica's eyes go wide. "That's it? We're done? You came all this way just for that?"

I get up from the table. "Do they have to-go boxes? And yes, I needed to see what she pulled off the cameras, and I had to tweak the algorithm in person. This laptop has never once been connected to the internet, and it never will be."

Zuzanna tucks the machine into her backpack. "I can ask about the boxes."

"Wait." The command in Anjelica's voice has us both freezing. "You had me come along to provide insight. Well, my gut tells me this is all too quick. Fuchs knows the city is covered in cameras. So if he's here, he'd avoid them."

"Yes, but that's impossible to do," Zuzanna says.

I know she's right, but Anjelica's latched onto something. My niggling doubts maybe.

"We should at least go see his childhood home," Anjelica says. "What if one of the neighbors recognized him when your cameras didn't?"

She has a point. But that means finding the neighbors and speaking to them. Not just flipping through camera images on the computer.

"I can take you to his childhood home," Zuzanna offers.

"You know where it is?" Anjelica asks.

Zuzanna shrugs. "He's famous here."

Anjelica makes an amused noise. "Well, he's infamous where we're from."

"All right," I say. "Let's go then."

Somehow I know Fuchs isn't here. It's not the cameras or the results from the search program—it's more of a lack of prickling on my skin. Irrational, inexplicable, and completely psychosomatic, but still present. Or rather, not.

I'm going to find Fuchs, but it won't be here.

CHAPTER 9

We've found the house—a modest, one-story structure in a part of town known as Polska Nowa Wieś—and we've even found some neighbors. Specifically, an elderly man who very much remembers the Fuchses.

"They were always a bit"—he twists his finger through the air to mime something floating away—"above it all, I suppose."

He's telling us this in heavily accented English. When Zuzanna offered to translate, he refused with an offended frown. His English is fine; it's just taking me a few seconds to process the words through his accent.

Anjelica seems to immediately understand him though. "Is that why they moved away?"

He shrugs with his entire body, even his face getting in on the motion. "Probably. But things weren't so good after the communists fell. They were a family who thought they deserved good things."

There's no malice in his voice—it's like he's telling a story about someone long dead. The Fuchses have been gone so long and he stayed, so maybe they kind of are to him.

When people left the children's home—staff, other kids—

they almost never came back. I couldn't blame them, but still…

After about the tenth time, you learn to stop missing them. Or at least I did.

"But this place is beautiful," Anjelica says, sounding offended on his behalf.

"I keep my house up." The man turns, points to the end of the street. "See that pear tree there?"

I couldn't have told you it was a pear tree—how can you tell?—but I nod anyway.

"Everyone takes from that pear tree. It belongs to no one. When the pears are ripe, you take what you like, leave the rest for others to enjoy."

He says it like a poem. It makes me think of late-summer days, heavy heat, dripping juice. Bare skin.

My gaze finds Anjelica's legs, long, slim, wrapped in those stockings. They're not bare—those stockings are a peep show.

The tree. I need to focus on the tree.

There's a low fence around it, maybe to protect it from dogs. Or maybe for decoration. Behind it is a high hedge and no sign of what might be behind that.

"That *boy*"—the way the man twists that word tells me exactly who he's talking about—"would take every one. As soon as they were ripe, he'd fill buckets with them in the dead of night. A thief. A thief of what was freely given. And he'd cycle to the main market square and sell them."

Anjelica gasps. But me, I'm not surprised. That sounds just like Fuchs. I wonder if he ever ate any of the fruit or if he kept every piece to sell, all for more profit. Probably kept it.

My childhood taught me to know better than to touch what wasn't mine. That was a good way to get the shit kicked out of you, especially if it was a bigger, meaner kid. Now that I've made it, I acquire whatever I want. And then I can do anything I like with it.

I wouldn't take this free fruit, not from someone who really wants it, but I bet Fuchs would be out there at midnight if he were here. And not because he needed the money but just to prove he could.

"Have you seen him here?" I ask.

The man shakes his head. "No, not since he was a boy. They never came back once they left. Not even to visit family. Although you'd think he might want to visit his tree."

"His tree?" Anjelica is frowning.

"Oh yes, he bought the tree—and the land around it— many years ago." He gestures to the low fence around the tree, which I'd thought was to protect it. But I can see now it's to keep people out.

"So no one can eat the fruit?" Anjelica asks.

The man spits on the ground. "We take it anyway."

"Good." Anjelica crosses her arms. "Take all of it. Don't let a single pear rot on the ground."

The man laughs. I think he's more than half in love with Anjelica, which I can't blame him for. "My wife preserves them. I'll give you a jar."

Anjelica's face lights up. I notice I'm not included in the gift.

"If you see him," I say, handing over my card, "please call or email. Don't tell him we were here."

The man tucks the card into his pocket without looking at it. I figure it will go through the wash with those pants and disappear into oblivion. Maybe his wife is more responsible.

The wife doesn't seem more responsible, but I hand her a card anyway. She presses a jar of pears onto Anjelica, chats with her through Zuzanna, and before I can get too itchy, we're out the door and back on the road to Kraków.

"Well, that was informative," Anjelica says, the jar of pears nestled in her lap.

"I suppose." I blink away the afterimage of her legs, which is pressing into my eyelids. "We know he's not there."

"Beyond that, I meant. We know that he's always had a compulsion to... to..."

"Screw people over?"

"That and..." She taps her bottom lip, which is fire-engine red. I know that it's a pale pinkish berry color beneath, because of that one time I saw her without her makeup. "I don't know, I can't think of the word I want. Maybe there isn't one."

"Asshole doesn't cover it?"

"No. I mean, a lot of kids would take more pears than they meant to eat, waste a lot—that's normal kid stuff. But to sneak over in the dead of night, take them all, and then sell them? That's..." But she still can't find the word she wants.

I see what she means now. It's a special kind of selfishness, an intense almost jealousy, that would push a kid to do that. Anyone to do that.

I've met kids—lived with kids—who'd steal all kinds of stuff. They'd get caught, get beat if it was another kid's stuff, but they couldn't stop. This isn't that.

"It's fucked up," I say.

She nods like I've found the exact right words. I don't think I have, but if she's happy, I'm happy.

We drive in silence for a while longer. And then I hear a smack of lips, a moan of appreciation.

She's gotten into the pears, and she's eating them, juice dripping down her hand, coating her lips. When she swallows, her eyes close like she's just had a secret orgasm.

I snap my gaze back to the road and jerk the wheel, bringing the car back into our lane. Jesus fuck, what is she doing?

My heart is out of control. I can feel my pulse between my fingers.

"These are delicious." She's eating another one, and I absolutely cannot look—not if I want to keep the car on the road.

I glance over anyway. This time she's holding a slice out to me, palest gold and gleaming with juice.

"I'm driving." It sounds lame, but my brain is smoking into ruin.

She doesn't drop her hand. "They're really good."

I can't lose my focus on my driving, but I also can't look away from her. We're going to smash into a telephone pole because of a goddamn pear. Well, because Anjelica is so fucking hot holding out a pear to me.

Her fingers dip, waving the fruit in front of me. There's a scent of sugar and muted sunlight. "Don't you want some of Fuchs's fruit?"

The tease in her voice sends a bolt of heat straight to my cock. And she's half smiling like that's exactly what she intended.

When she puts it like that, I can't resist: I bend my head, wrap my mouth around the slice—and her fingers—and take it on my tongue. Her fingers are firm, warm compared to the soft chill of the pear.

She does a quiet noise halfway between a squeal and a gasp, like she never expected that.

And she never expected to like it so much.

My cock twitches even as my heart does a triumphant fist pump. I chew slowly, letting the flavor run between my teeth. She's right—it's a damn good pear, even preserved as it is.

I swallow it, running my tongue over my teeth to get every last drop. "Thanks. It was good."

She looks good with her lips parted, her hand still in the air between us. I could dip my head, lick the rest of the juice off her fingers. I could, and given her earlier reaction, she'd be just fine with it.

And then the car would run off the road, smash into something, and we could both die.

"You're welcome?" She drops her hand, looking shell-shocked. Her fingers stay pressed together as if she can't let go of something.

Then she gives herself a shake, seems to wake up. And very firmly puts the lid back on the jar.

Which of course I'm grateful for. I need to concentrate on my driving. Not her.

CHAPTER 10

I've only just met Helen a few days ago, but I already love her. She's passionate, enthusiastic, determined; but she also has a dream. When I was imagining my perfect first start-up founder, she was it.

"And here're the latest specs on the encryption." She pulls up a screen on her laptop. "Through some clever code, Jena has managed to make the users' data even more secure."

I'll have to ask Finn and January their opinions, but what I see here looks good. I might not be a programmer, but I've picked some things up. I smile at her. "You anticipated my next question. User security is going to always have to be one of your biggest priorities."

"I know." She beams back at me.

Helen's anticipated all my questions, showing me how much sleeker, more secure, the app is. She's anticipated all of them except one, the biggest one.

"What's the user-base growth look like?"

Her smile flickers, freezes. "The past few weeks haven't been great." For a moment I suspect she's about to try to bull-shit her way through this, but then she brings up the next slide. "Trial subscriptions are down. Way down."

The data she's showing me is grim. Since the app won't

use advertising, it has to get paying subscribers. And the way to do that is to give them a free trial where they'll fall in love with the app and want to pay.

But people aren't even signing up for the free trial. Which means they're not signing up for subscriptions. There's no way the company will even come close to their projected growth targets like this.

"What does your marketing person say about this?"

"She thinks it's a blip. Nothing to worry about."

I look up sharply at the hitch in her tone. "But you don't."

"I'm not going to brush it off as a blip," she says firmly. "I'm meeting with her today about new marketing strategies to address it."

That's encouraging. But the downward-trending line she's shown me keeps nagging at me. What if Finn is right and their growth just isn't going to happen? "And if it doesn't turn out to be a blip? And the new marketing plan doesn't fix it?"

To her credit, Helen doesn't flinch. "We hold back on the development of new features. Focus on the parts our subscribers already love and improve those. Cutting... cutting the new positions if we need to."

It's a hard choice she's describing, to decide what to kill when something's failing. Don't cut back and you'll run out of money. Cut back too much and you'll never grow the company like you need to. And those are real people she'll have to fire if it comes to that. Lives will be injured if she has to let people go.

It's a rare start-up that comes back from something like that. But I have faith Helen will turn this around. It's why I invested in her.

"Good," I say. "Let me know what comes out of the marketing meeting. And keep me updated on the new subscriber numbers. If this is just a blip, I want to know. And if it's not..."

I don't have to spell the rest out for her. She nods, then rises smartly. "Definitely. I'll be in touch."

Once she's gone, I rub at my temples, staring at the calming sight of my atrium. The meeting went great, but I'm not used to being the person behind the desk, not yet. Helen's looking to me to be the authority, to hand her the answers along with the money. Or at least to pretend I could if she needed them. I'm sure I'll get better at this as I go along, but these first meetings are exhausting. And I've got two more of them this week.

My assistant comes in then, smiling and holding a steaming cup of tea. "I figured you'd need this." Georgia was my assistant before this, and she knows me too well, thank goodness.

"I do. Thank you." As I take the cup from her, she unloads several folders filled with prospectuses from under her arm and onto my desk. I groan. "Did I really ask to read all these?"

"You did." She's chirpy, which I used to like, back when I was only the office manager. Now her cheer is making me cranky. But that's just me being crabby about all this reading I've brought on myself. "I pulled out every one that matched your specifications."

I start flipping through the one on top. I'm instantly energized by what I see. Another start-up with a female founder, this time working on mobile games. Most people don't realize women play tons of computer games—but mostly on their phones. The gaming industry sneers at them as not being worth their time, but it's an untapped market. Just look at *Candy Crush* and its five million variants.

"This is exactly what I was looking for," I tell Georgia, pointing to the folder. I pick up the tea. "And this was exactly what I needed."

"Well, no more meetings today," Georgia says, "and there's the call with WamaSpec at three. Want me to make sure you're not disturbed until then?"

I'm caught up short by that. Back when I wasn't a partner, I had to always be ready for disturbances. That was my whole job—to clean up disturbances before they reached the Bastards.

But now I'm the one to be protected from all that. It's nice… but also a touch unnerving, because I was really good at running interference.

"Yes," I say slowly. "That would be great." Hours and hours of uninterrupted reading time with a hot cup of tea. What a treat. "Don't let anyone in. Unless it's one of the partners. Um, is Dev here today by any chance?"

Georgia isn't fooled by my stumbling attempts at casualness. "I haven't seen him. Not since you guys came back from Europe."

Neither have I, and since it's only been two days, I shouldn't be worried. Dev sometimes disappears, either into his work or his office. That's just how he is.

I'd usually send someone to check on him after a few days though. But that's Yancy's job now.

My fingers tingle with the urge to do… something. Maybe even check on him myself. Just to see him…

"Do you want me to find him?" Georgia is looking at me strangely, and I realize I never responded to her.

"No, it's fine. I was only curious." I look through the folder again. "And yeah, no interruptions until three."

Georgia nods and leaves. I read through more prospectuses, start to put together some notes for Helen, and think way too much about Dev. Does he think our trip to Poland was a waste? Does he regret telling me about his past? Or is there something smaller, more innocent to explain why he's disappeared?

And where should we go to look for Fuchs next?

There's a knock at my door a little after two. I look up, expecting it to be Georgia with something that can't wait, but it's Logan. He's holding two coffees from Roasted.

"I thought you could use an afternoon pick-me-up." He sets the cups on my desk, then pulls a bar of chocolate out of his suit jacket. "And a treat."

I take both the offerings gratefully. "This is perfect. I met with my very first start-up founder today."

"Oh? How'd it go?"

"Great. She's so excited and ready to do some disrupting. I loved it."

Logan smiles, which makes him even more handsome. Really, one man shouldn't be that good-looking. It puts the rest of humanity at a disadvantage. "That sounds awesome. I can't wait to see what they come up with."

"Me too. And I've already got a few more companies I want to look at. There's just so much I've been wanting to do…" I flick through one of the prospectuses. "And so much to get done."

"Remember to pace yourself," Logan says. "Burnout is real."

He should know—he used to work like a maniac. Then Callie left him and he was forced to reassess everything.

"I thrive on having too much to do." One look at my social schedule proves that. "And I'm even leaving early tonight for my book club meeting."

"Good. Don't lose any of the things that make you happy." His expression turns sober. "This trip you and Dev took to Europe… What was that about?"

I set down the coffee. This suddenly feels less like a spontaneous treat and more like a bribe. "He didn't tell you?"

"He doesn't tell us much of anything these days." Logan's voice has chilled to match the temperature of mine. "But he seems to still trust you."

Yes, he does. My instinct is to tell Logan what I can— maybe not everything about Dev's past but at least about our hunt for Fuchs. But I also don't want to betray Dev's trust. If I'm all he's got right now, and he thinks I've betrayed him…

"You should ask him," I say, biting my lip. God, but this feels awful to stonewall Logan like this. If only Dev would stop being stupid and simply confess everything, we could all go back to how things used to be.

But he won't do that. He's decided he can't trust the Bastards. Maybe he never really did.

My blurting out his secrets for him isn't going to fix things either. Why does he have to be so closed off and infuriating? And why am I so damn attracted to him in spite of it?

"I would," Logan says, "but he hasn't been around since you guys got back. Considering that company resources were used, it would be nice to know what the trip was for." His brows draw together and he leans toward me. "Anjie, if he's in trouble, you can tell us. I don't care what it is. We'll help."

I blink hard and swallow. Does Dev know what he's rejecting when he pushes these guys away? "He's not in trouble. I swear it's nothing like that."

"Is it about his family? His childhood?"

My heart trips. Of course Logan would see right to that. He's the details guy, and there are zero details about Dev's childhood.

"Um, you have to ask him." My clumsy answer is pretty much a yes, but I can't outright lie.

Logan stares me down. "But he's been to Poland before," he says, mostly to himself. "So why go with you this time?"

"Look, I can't—"

"Did you meet his family?"

I sigh and fold my hands. "This isn't my story to tell. You —all of you—need to sit down with Dev and work this out. But no, I didn't meet his family."

Some of the intensity in Logan's face fades. "You're worried about him too."

"Of course I am. But I can't *make* him do anything."

Logan laughs at the frustration in my voice. "You can't manage him and it infuriates you." He stops laughing. "You never tried to set him up with anyone."

Oh boy. "I never set you up with anyone either."

He runs his tongue over his teeth. "Okay, well, you *interfere.* Very precisely and very effectively. And you did it for all of us. Except Dev."

My skin runs hot, then cold. I can't tell what Logan is getting at. Or maybe I can and I don't want to go there. "I like playing matchmaker. And none of you are complaining now."

Thinking of Dev with another woman, one I've seen would be perfect for him… It makes me go cold and hot all at once, like I'm getting sick.

"No," Logan says, "we all appreciate what you did. We, uh, we always kind of suspected you and Dev had something going on. He talked about you before we hired you. He's never talked about anybody since."

Okay, I'm just going to meet this head-on. "There might've been an attraction, but we never acted on it."

"I wasn't accusing—"

I keep talking over him. "But there's nothing between us. And there won't be."

I'm resolved on that, even after learning about his childhood—and that he still kisses like a dream. He's not ready for a relationship. He might never be. That hasn't changed. He definitely isn't ready for a family, and that isn't likely to ever change.

Imagining Dev holding a baby makes my heart squeeze so tight it hurts.

Logan looks like he has more to say, but he keeps his mouth shut. "Ah" is all that comes out. A small noise of resigned understanding. "Sorry. I won't ask again."

"It's okay. I'm sure you were all curious. And we both agree it's for the best. We're friends."

I don't know if those last two are true, especially after

Dev ate that pear out of my hand, but I want to ease Logan's mind.

I've eased my own mind in telling Logan all this. It feels good to tell him, to admit that yes, there was something between Dev and me but nothing more serious is going on. It's like opening the curtains and letting the sun in on our friendship.

Again, I can't understand how Dev can hide away from this. Being open and honest with someone who cares about you just feels right.

"Good," Logan says. "We all want you to be happy. If you're cool with it—and him—then we're all cool."

He doesn't say he wants Dev to be happy though. Or ask if Dev is cool with our situation.

"Really, you should talk to Dev." They all need to sit down and just clear the air. I wish I could simply set up a meeting, put Emotional Outpouring on the schedule, and have them get down to it. But my powers only go so far.

"Sure," Logan says as he gets up. "He knows where to find us."

My heart sinks. That's not what I wanted to hear. They have to go to Dev since he doesn't seem likely to go to them.

Then I want to grind my teeth. If they weren't such stubborn bastards... then they wouldn't be the Bastards I know and love.

"And you know where to find him," I call as Logan leaves.

"Except he hasn't been in his office for days," Logan says as he closes the door behind him.

Which makes me worry all over again about Dev's absence and how to fix... everything.

CHAPTER 11

"Where the hell have you been?"

I blink up at Anjelica, who's towering over my desk, her hands on her hips. She's beautifully angry, her eyes flashing and her color high.

"I'm sorry?" I can't think what I've done to piss her off. But then I can't really think at all with how her chest is rising and falling, her lips parted and gleaming, and—

"I can't believe you." She crosses her arms under her breasts, which doesn't help matters.

I lean back in my chair, forcing myself to be cold, calm. "I have no idea what you're upset about."

"I just said."

I replay our conversation. "You're mad that I was gone? But someone came by with food and everything, said they were sent by the firm. I figured someone knew where I was."

She waits, as if it's totally reasonable for her to be angry about it even though she's literally never cared before. I once disappeared into my apartment for a month—there was this coding problem I just couldn't let go of—and she didn't say anything about it. There was a junior associate coming over and bugging me every other day and food deliveries I don't remember ordering, but not Anjelica.

Fuck. The realization breaks over me like a storm cloud. "It was you."

She doesn't play dumb. "Of course it was me! You'd die if someone wasn't checking up on you. And while you may not care about us, we care about you."

"I care about you." I say it quietly, simply. Not cold. Not blank.

She presses her lips tightly together. "I got worried. I mean, I usually get worried when you just disappear, but I was really worried this time. After Poland... I didn't know what you were thinking."

I was thinking about her offering me that slice of pear mostly. My lips on her knuckles, my tongue brushing her fingertip, the sweet stickiness of the juice... and the noise she made while her fingers were in my mouth.

She was probably thinking mostly about the tree though. Fuchs being a little shit about the tree didn't bother me as much as it did her.

"I was working on something else." Can she hear the hitch in my voice? "An algorithm for a start-up I invested in. I tend to lose track of things when I'm doing that."

She unwinds her arms, then sits in a chair. "Logan asked what we were doing in Poland."

"What did he say when you told him?"

"I didn't." She's not happy about it. Every part of her is tense.

But she didn't tell him. I... I have no idea what to make of that. I just assumed Anjelica would tell them we were looking for Fuchs, then come up with some explanation for why. And I wouldn't have to do anything.

But she didn't. She chose to keep my secrets.

"What did you tell him?"

"That he had to talk to you."

She punted the problem right back into my lap. I almost smile. "And what did he say?"

"That you know where to find him."

That sounds right. They've all been keeping their distance from me, their anger at what I've done hardening into a chilled wall.

"So?" she demands. "Are you going to find him and talk to him?"

"Of course." I don't say when that will happen. "Where should we go next to find Fuchs?"

She arranges her skirt over her knees with short, sharp movements. She's still upset with me, but she's holding back. "I don't know. The family came to Chicago, and he grew up there."

I suppose if we're retracing Fuchs's life from the beginning, it makes sense to visit Chicago next. But neither of his parents are alive, and I don't know what his former classmates and neighbors might tell us. Poland wasn't exactly illuminating.

"He really got his start at Stanford," I say. "That's where he met Hanult."

Hanult is probably a bigger piece of Fuchs's life than even his parents. Every interview or profile of Fuchs mentions him—the professor who saw a spark in the young student and nurtured it. Hanult introduced Fuchs to his first big investors, got him connections in the tech world, and started him on his course to world domination.

Hanult's also dead, which complicates things. But there are plenty of people in Silicon Valley who knew him.

"Not Chicago," I say. "We can fly there if no other leads work out. Stanford is right around the corner though; I know someone who went to Stanford with Fuchs, was in his class with Hanult."

She taps her fingers against her thigh. "I don't agree. Look at how much we learned in Poland. Ohio might give us even more."

"What did we learn in Poland? Besides that Fuchs was born a jerk."

Her face is full of exasperated pity. I'm reminded all over again that I don't react like I ought to. That I don't know how to act around people still, especially her.

"We learned a ton." She starts to tick off on her fingers. "Fuchs has always been over-the-top possessive. He won't hesitate to steal what isn't his. And he remembers a slight. Always."

That was kind of apparent from our interactions with him in the past year, but she's right—it's more clear how deep all that goes with him.

"I can't stop thinking about him taking all those pears." Anjelica's gaze is unfocused, like she's staring at a memory. "It would have never even occurred to me to do something like that. And my parents—"

She shuts her mouth so hard my heart jumps. "You okay?"

"It's fine." She waves her hand, makes herself smile. "I was having some problems with my family back when we met. But we started working them out a few years ago. Things are good, but sometimes bad memories still come up."

I can't formulate a response to that. There's nothing in my past like that to connect to, to offer up to her as commiseration. "I'm sorry" is the best I can do.

She seems satisfied with it though. "Don't be. Things are good now. And my parents would have been so appalled and ashamed if I'd stolen all those pears and sold them. Why didn't Fuchs's parents react the same?"

I can think of a lot of reasons, and I don't even have parents. "They didn't care. They wanted the money. They approved. They didn't know."

Anjelica shakes her head. "They had to know. The pears are all gone, he's suddenly got all this money? Parents always suspect something."

Do they? You were always under suspicion in the group

home, but it was more of a general blanket accusation. *If you're here, something's gone wrong. What else is going to go wrong with you?*

"He's an only child," Anjelica says. "Maybe they spoiled him."

I'd sometimes get asked if I was an only child, which I never knew how to answer. I suppose I was, except that wasn't what they meant. They wanted to know if I was the sole focus of my parents' love. If I learned to fight and share and love with my siblings.

None of those things were true about me.

"Or maybe they couldn't stop him." If Fuchs treated his parents the way he treats the rest of the world, as nothing more than obstacles to his will, I wouldn't be surprised. "But the spoiling idea also makes sense. Are you an only child?"

She's never mentioned siblings, and suddenly I'm curious. I never ask anyone else about their family to avoid questions about my own, but I know Anjelica won't do that. So I'm free to ask with her. It's… nice.

"Um, kind of. It's hard to explain." She presses a crease of her skirt between her fingers. "There was a family next door to us with a kid my age. We practically grew up together."

"Ah." I had bunkmates, people I'd even call friends, but no one I'd say grew up with me. "Does your family still live there? And the other family too?"

This is a world I thought only existed on TV, of tight-knit neighbors and families, of people putting roots in one place and staying there. And Anjelica lived it. Something deeper than fascination burns in my chest.

She drops her skirt, places her palms flat on her thighs. "Yes, my parents are still in the same house. The other family gave their house to their kid, so I suppose they still live there in a way."

She's too rigid. Something's wrong about this. "Do you still talk to her?"

Anjelica's face settles into a mask. "It's a he. And no, we lost touch. My parents tell me about him though."

This is all wrong. It should be an idyllic story of lifelong childhood friends, but there's something very painful beneath it. And I haven't the faintest idea of how to unearth it. Not that I even have the right—Anjelica doesn't want me poking through her past any more than I want her poking in mine.

But I also want to understand. This is Anjelica—I want to understand her more deeply than I do myself.

The realization locks up my chest. I've been attracted to her for years—her mind, her body, the innate sparkle of her —but this is more than attraction.

Maybe this is what they call longing. Real longing.

I swallow, making my face still, my expression clear. She said no. My longing or whatever it is can't be her problem. Not until she's ready to say yes.

Judging by the pear incident, that might be sooner than she thinks.

"I see," I say, putting all my unspoken understanding into it. "I don't keep up with anyone from my childhood."

It's more than I've confessed to anyone except her. The words come off my tongue awkwardly, but once they're out, they don't feel so bad.

"Is there anyone you wanted to keep up with?" Her gaze is gentle but penetrating.

I try to think of someone. There were so many people, kids and adults, who came and went. Kids with problems that ran deep, adults with too many kids to help and too little time. I search for the bright spots in my dusty memories.

"Mr. Jarvis was cool." I stare at the desktop, polished to a high sheen, as I remember. "He was my high school shop teacher."

I was good at math—I was a genius at math—but the math teachers didn't have time for a genius. They encouraged me, but I didn't need their help, so they spent their time on the kids who did. I never blamed them.

Mr. Jarvis was different. I was awkward at shop, at taking time and care with things. Math was easy, so I breezed through it, and everything else bored me, so I didn't do it. Shop class was something entirely else. Mr. Jarvis didn't let me breeze through or quit.

Anjelica is watching with an expectant look, waiting for me to go on. So I tell her exactly what I just remembered. The words feel less awkward as they keep coming, and it helps that she doesn't interrupt. By the end I feel… lighter. Not better necessarily, but definitely different.

"He might still be teaching," she says. "You could look him up if you want."

There's no pressure in her tone, which I appreciate. I can take or leave her offer.

"It's been years," I say. "He won't remember me."

She lifts one eyebrow in disbelief. "Even if he doesn't remember you, he'd probably be happy to hear from you. Teachers love to know they're fondly remembered."

Suddenly the lightness is gone and a weight is settling on my chest. If I remember so much about him and he doesn't remember me at all… I don't want to know about it. "We need to find someone who knew Professor Hanult, not Mr. Jarvis," I say. "Fuchs is still out there."

Disappointment flickers over her face, but she quickly squashes it. "You said you knew someone. I don't know anybody at Stanford."

There's a wistfulness there that irritates me. "It's not everything it's cracked up to be. The personal connections are more valuable than the education there in my opinion."

She shrugs. "A lot of people haven't heard of USD. At least the Cal States are kind of famous."

I snort. "They're not. Nobody outside California can seem to understand they're not part of the UC system."

We share a smile of sympathy.

"Did you like college?" she asks.

The way people talk about their college experiences never really resonated with me. They go on about being independent, doing whatever they want, meeting new people, and partying. I've been pretty much independent my entire life, so that wasn't anything novel, meeting new people wasn't exciting to me, and since I was paying for the education, there wasn't time to party.

"I liked their machine shop," I say. "It was much nicer than my high school one."

She rocks a foot back and forth. "I loved the campus. It was on top of a hill and very beautiful. It was..." Her voice dies as her expression goes sad. Almost unbearably so. "It was nice to look at pretty things at times."

I want to reach out to her, to touch her arm or hand, to let her know she's not alone. It's what she'd do for anyone else. I also want to know what happened to make her so sad, and I want to make it right.

I keep my hands where they are. "I'll call my friend." My words feel too blunt in the moment, but I can't take them back. "I'll see if he can meet this week, and we can ask him about Fuchs."

Anjelica squares her shoulders, clears her throat. The sadness is gone as quickly as it came. "Right. We should ask about friends he might be staying with, old girlfriends, or even places he talked about going one day."

"And Hanult," I say. "There may be a clue in their relationship. I think he's the only person that ever really got close to Fuchs."

She gives me an odd look as she gets up. "There are probably other people he was close to even if it doesn't seem that way." Before she leaves, she wags a finger at me. "Don't disappear again. And you need to tell the other guys... something. That's not my job."

"Don't worry about it."

I'm not planning on telling them everything, but I can come up with something. At least enough to get them to leave Anjelica alone. While I'm touched she kept my secrets, that's not really her job either.

CHAPTER 12

Even though I won't have time to go home and change, I arrive early for my Tuesday-night meeting with Dev. It means I'm still in my dance-instructor gear—workout clothes, hair in a ponytail, sneakers on my feet. It's strange to be without heels, but after an hour of dancing in them, I have to give my feet a break.

I look perfectly fine, but it feels weird to be dressed like this. What I have to share with him is worth it though.

Dev's chosen a coffee cart on the Stanford campus for the meeting. The cart itself is closed up for the night, but the tables and chairs are out, the deep yellow of the streetlamps illuminating the lawns and trees surrounding us. A few students walk by, taking no notice of me.

People always do a double take when they see me out of my usual clothes, like I've switched faces or something. Dev does not do that. His expression is steady, unchanging as I walk up to him.

My heart goes fluttery. My body can't help but react to him. Especially my heart. With everything that he's begun to share with me, it's gotten even worse.

I wonder if he contacted his high school teacher. I doubt it. Just the fact that Dev even told me about Mr. Jarvis is a major, major thing… but I want more for him. I've always wanted more for him. That he doesn't want more for himself is the central issue between us.

"Everything okay?" he asks as he holds out a chair for me. I told him at the last minute that I needed to see him before we met with his friend, so he's probably worried.

"It's fine." I reach into my workout bag, pull out stacks of paper. "I have a surprise for you."

He squints at the long list of addresses, running his finger down them. "What is this?"

"It's the address of every property owned by Corvus, its subsidiaries, and Arne Fuchs."

There're well over a thousand addresses on there, and some were tricky to track down, especially the international ones, but the list is more or less complete. Fuchs's hiding spot has got to be on that list somewhere.

Dev's mouth curls up into a slow smile. The pride and pleasure in it makes me glow. "How did you find all these?"

I shrug. "Elbow grease mostly. The information is all there, somewhere, it just needed to be gathered up." I point to an address he's about to flip past. "That one is the tree."

Dev frowns at it. "Why would a tree have an address?"

"Every parcel of land has to be marked off somehow. I guess when he bought it, the tree was given an address."

He taps a finger on the stack. "There're too many to personally, physically check them all."

Good Lord, he couldn't have possibly wanted to do that. "We just have to go through them systematically, using what we know about him. I mean, he's not going to choose some random office building in Anchorage as a hiding spot."

"He owns a building in Anchorage?"

"He owns buildings everywhere," I say. "We have to figure out which properties actually have meaning for him." I gesture to the addresses. "Like the pear tree in Poland."

Dev pushes the papers to the side and leans toward me.

"Not everyone runs back to their past. This might all be a waste of time."

"Fuchs didn't jump fully formed from business school. His past dictates what he'll do now. He's always been a greedy, grasping jerk. So even when he's hiding, he's still going to be looking to take something. Or maybe to be reminded of a past victory." I nod slowly. "Yeah, he's going to want some kind of trophy while he licks his wounds. And plots his comeback."

Dev's skeptical. "Okay, but how can we get that from these addresses?"

"Context." I nod at the man coming toward us.

Dev rises in one fluid motion, reaching out to shake the man's hand. "Riley. Thanks for meeting us."

Riley shakes my hand next. "My pleasure." His smile is a touch flirty.

"Anjelica." I don't give him my nickname, and I keep the handshake brief.

Dev looks at both of us coolly. "Anjelica is the newest partner at Bastard Capital." There's a hint of warning there.

Recognition dawns on Riley's face, and when he sits down, he leans away from me. Thank goodness.

"So, you want to know everything about Arne." Riley crosses his legs as he sprawls in the chair. "Dude was always kind of odd."

"Were you two friends?" I ask.

Riley ponders that. "Arne never really had close friends. He saw everyone as competition, although he could be friendly. Just as long as he didn't see you as a threat."

"Threats? In college?" Dev raises an eyebrow.

"Yeah. Like I said, he was competitive. Over grades, internships, everything. Someone else getting an A might have no effect on his grade, but he didn't see things that way."

"Did he see you as a threat?" I ask.

"No, which is why we were friendly." Riley smiles. "I had a

job waiting for me at Rhodes Partners the entire time, so I didn't care. I just needed a degree and the connections, you know?"

Dev's jaw tightens, but he doesn't say anything.

"Did Arne ever talk about places he wanted to go? Things he wanted to see?"

Riley might be privileged, but he's not dumb. "Not really. What's that got to do with breaking up Corvus?"

"We're trying to account for all his real estate holdings," Dev says smoothly. "He put some personal real estate under Corvus's name, and he was very secretive. There's a lot to untangle."

Riley nods. "Hell yeah, he was always secretive. Like worried you'd steal his ideas for problem sets, accusing people of copying off him. Which is ridiculous. It's an assignment; we're all going to do it the same way pretty much."

"Was he exceptionally smart or inventive?" I ask.

Riley ponders that. "He could convince other people he was, which is almost the same thing."

We all sit with that for a moment.

"What about Hanult?" I ask. "Fuchs managed to convince him of his special genius."

Riley laughs. "Those two were something. It was like they were both acting out some movie with Hanult as the wise, older mentor and Fuchs the brash kid needing inspiration and direction. Hanult thought Fuchs should be running the world, and Fuchs agreed."

"Was Fuchs close with anyone else in school? Students, professors?" Dev asks.

"Like he was with Hanult?" Riley shakes his head. "Fuchs wasn't dumb. He didn't alienate people, but you could tell he thought of them as things to be used. He was over at Hanult's house all the time though."

My memory jogs at the mention of the professor's house.

"Really? Was that usual for students to go to professors' houses?"

"Sure, for the networking opportunities," Riley says. "The professors knew the guys you needed to know in the tech world—CEOs, VCs. Some of them liked to throw parties, show off who they knew. You'd be stupid not to take advantage. But Fuchs would go over to Hanult's just to hang out. Like I said, part of their mentor/protégé act."

I never got invited over to a professor's house in college— it just wasn't even a thing we considered. I guess none of my professors had really powerful friends they wanted to show off.

"He never had any cofounders with Corvus," Dev says to me. "It was always him alone."

I nod, because I see where he's going with this, then turn back to Riley. "So the only meaningful relationship he made at Stanford was with Hanult?"

"As far as I can tell," Riley says. "He was always a weird guy though." He frowns, taps a knuckle against the table. "I don't see how any of this helps with Corvus and real estate."

No, he can't see how it helps because he doesn't know about the address list. I think I've stumbled onto something big.

I lean toward him, my expression earnest. "It actually helps a lot. Trust us."

Riley turns on the charm. "Great. Good. Anything else you want to know?"

"No, I think that's it," Dev says dryly. He holds out his hand. "Thanks."

Riley shakes his hand, then mine. "Happy to help. I owe you because of"—he glances at me—"because of the *thing*. So we're even."

"We are."

Once he's gone, I turn to Dev. "What thing?"

His mouth flattens, and it seems for a moment he won't

93

answer. When he does, the words come out stiffly. "His dad gave him some money to invest a few years ago, and Riley completely fucked it up because he actually knows nothing about finance. He came to me, begging for help. So I sorted it all out. Naturally he didn't want anyone to know he's not the financial wizard he pretends to be."

I narrow my eyes. Dev's always doing that, pulling out some tidbit he knows about someone or calling in a favor from people we've never met. And never showing anyone exactly how he does it.

This story about Riley might explain a lot of those instances.

"How many people owe you favors?"

"Everyone has secrets in the tech world. I happen to know a lot of those secrets."

A bleak chill runs over my skin. He was almost robotic when he said that. "You sound like Fuchs."

"He's not wrong about that." His tone is brisk, on the edge of contemptuous. "I was able to acquire his company because of favors I was owed. Secrets I know. This place runs on power, not kindness. And I wasn't going to win against him without using some of his own tactics."

I don't think I've ever heard him so cold, so calculating before. "Tactics like hurting people?"

He sucks in a sharp, angry breath. "No," he bites out. "I don't do that. And you know it."

Maybe I do and maybe I don't. Maybe I'm only just beginning to know him. What he's saying right now... is frightening. Not like how I thought he was.

"You hurt the Bastards," I point out quietly. He might not have meant to hurt them, but he did.

There might be a flicker of something in his eyes, but it's gone too fast to tell. "They're big boys."

"Men can have hurt feelings too." He's acting like everyone's as unemotional and detached as he pretends to be. But it's too late for him to pretend with me. "Did you have a professor like that in college?" I ask. "Or anyone you were close to?"

We've just heard about how even Fuchs had friends and a mentor—Dev must have something like that.

"No," he says with more than a hint of triumph. Like he's proved I'm wrong about men and their feelings. "I went to class, did my work, and went to my job. That's all."

"You don't feel like you missed out?" I gesture at the campus surrounding us. "College is supposed to be memorable. Where you make lifelong friends."

"Was it the best time of your life?" he shoots back.

My heart freezes. My mouth opens, closes, nothing coming out. "It wasn't," I finally say. "There were good parts—great parts—but…"

I can't finish. I can't tell Dev what Kaleb did, not when he's being so… so awful.

He glances at his hands, then looks fully at me. "I'm sorry." His expression is open, honest. "I was being a jerk."

I purse my lips. He was, and that's usually not like him. I guess I hit a nerve, not that it excuses him. "If you want people to share their stories," I say quietly, "you have to share some of yourself. A relationship is a two-way street."

"You'll share your college stories with me if I share…?" He cocks his head, puzzled. "Share what?"

"It's not a deal or tit-for-tat kind of thing."

He still doesn't understand. I don't tell him things in the hopes that he'll tell me things. I'm not keeping score or anything. That's not how relationships work.

But maybe he'll never learn any better. Maybe he can't.

"We didn't learn anything here," he says suddenly. He's done with memories and personal revelations and feelings. "Everything Riley said we already knew. It's not like Fuchs is hiding out on the campus."

I pull in a deep breath, my eyes widening. I almost forgot.

"No, we did get something." I start to flip through the addresses I brought. "Remember how he said Fuchs was at Hanult's house all the time?"

"Yeah. But Hanult is dead…" Realization dawns on his face. "Do you know his address?"

"Not for certain, but I remember there was a Palo Alto address in a residential area. I remember it because it stood out—why would he own a house there?" I point at one of the entries. "There. That's the one I remember."

Dev immediately pulls the address up on his map app. When he turns the screen to me, I see the house is right smack in the middle of a suburban development. Not exactly prime real estate for a tech company to be purchasing.

"How do we know it's Hanult's house?" Dev asks.

I shrug. "We don't. But it wouldn't hurt to go take a look."

Dev frowns, first at the map, then at me. "But why would he be there?"

"Because that's where he was told he could—should—take over the world. If he's planning a comeback, he's going to want that reassurance."

He's going to want to go back to the beginning, back when he was young and limitless and he thought nothing could hold him back.

Dev ponders that. "Fuchs doesn't really operate like a normal person though."

"Everyone likes to hear that they're special." I tap my finger against the page. "And it's only fifteen minutes away."

He grabs his keys. "Let's do it then."

CHAPTER 13

The house is dark, the windows blank when we pull up. The rest of the houses—all variations on the same pseudo-Tudor theme—have porch lights and interior lights gently, tastefully glowing, luxury cars tucked into the driveways. "We're home and no, you can't come in" they seem to say.

Hanult's house looks like no one's home, but there is a car in the driveway. A late-model Honda; practical, fuel efficient. Not at all flashy.

"I guess someone lives here," Anjelica says as I park. "But who?"

"That's what we're going to find out."

She grabs my arm. I ignore how that makes me feel. "We're just going to knock on the door?"

"That's what a door is for." My gut is telling me that Fuchs isn't there, but someone else very important is. My gut is usually always right. "If they tell us to leave, we will."

She releases my arm. The place where she touched continues to tingle. "If Fuchs is here, I suppose that's the entire point."

I nod, then open the door. "Let's see if we really are that lucky."

The moment I knock, an interior light switches on.

Someone must have seen the car and known we were coming up the drive.

When the door swings open, revealing who is in the house, I'm stunned. Knocked-down-to-my-toes stunned.

"You... I never thought you'd be here," I say to the woman holding the door open.

She's not so surprised to see me. "I figured it was a matter of time before you tracked me down."

"I've been trying." Talk about hiding in plain sight...

Anjelica stabs me with a look, then holds out her hand. "I'm Anjelica. With Bastard Capital."

"I'm Pippa." She shakes Anjelica's hand with a small smile. "Congratulations on the partnership."

"Thank you." Anjelica's polite expression slips. "Clearly you and Dev are already acquainted."

Pippa laughs and I clear my throat. "This is..." I stumble on the word to describe her. "Pippa was Arne's housekeeper."

"Among other things."

My gaze snaps to Pippa in surprise. That she was much more than Arne's housekeeper was a closely held secret. One that I discovered and used against Arne.

Pippa shrugs at my look. "He's gone. I don't owe him any more silence."

That answers the question of whether Fuchs is hiding out here. Damn it. I guess we weren't that lucky.

Anjelica is wide-eyed, shocked, but trying to hide it. "I... It's nice to meet you." That comes out with a weak wobble.

Pippa steps back into the entryway. "You should probably come in. We need to talk."

"Thanks." As Anjelica passes me, she glances up, her jaw tight, her skin pale. She's not happy with me.

Is she jealous? Or annoyed at the reveal of another of my secrets? I'm hoping it's jealousy—that'd be a promising development—but hope's never gotten me very far in life.

The interior of the house is very professor-modern—lots

of books, a few heavy pieces of furniture, and art so tasteful it's right on the edge of shocking. Or at least eyebrow-raising.

"Is this all the original furniture?" I ask as Pippa leads us into a sitting room.

She's got an almost ageless face where you can't tell if she's in her twenties, thirties, or even forties. At first glance she's not particularly striking, but there's some mystery lurking in her gray eyes that makes you look again. I suppose that mystery is what snared Fuchs. That and her profession.

"Yep." She folds herself into a chair, tucking her legs under her. "He was very insistent that everything remain as Professor Hanult left it."

"You live here?" Anjelica's perched on the edge of her chair.

Pippa shrugs. "It's a nice house. I wasn't going to turn it down, not in this real estate market."

Anjelica and I exchange a glance. Pippa perhaps doesn't know that I control this house now, not Arne.

"You heard about the takeover?" I ask.

"Of course." Pippa tips her chin up. "Why, have you come to evict me?"

Mockery rides lightly under her tone. She's not exactly shaking in her shoes. That was the appeal for Fuchs, I think. A woman who wasn't awed by him, who'd make him get on his knees. And since he was paying her, he could put her aside whenever he liked. No messy emotions to deal with.

"No." My own voice is soft. Pippa's being brave, but the prospect of losing your home would worry anyone. "I'll be signing over the title to you. Free and clear."

For a moment her mask drops and she lets herself be both shocked and delighted. "Oh. Wow."

"You've earned it."

Anjelica clears her throat, edging even farther out on the

chair. "Have you seen Fuchs lately? We're... We need to get in touch with him."

"No." Pippa's mask of amused boredom is back. "I'm surprised you didn't ask me sooner though."

"I didn't know you were here," I say. "His main house is completely empty. No one's taking care of it."

"He dismissed everyone once the news was public." She tilts her head. "Actually, he told us all to get out and not come back."

The spot above my eye begins to throb. Right. There're all those employees to take care of too. "Could you make a list of all the household employees and their information? I'll take care of back pay and references."

"So you were really his housekeeper?" Anjelica asks.

Pippa smiles. "I was. I was an executive before I became a domme, and running a household like that wasn't much different than running a department. He paid me well, so I was content."

Anjelica looks like she has a million more questions, all of them stuck in her throat.

"When did he put you in this house?" I ask.

She thinks about it. "Two years ago. I think it was empty before that."

"Did he ever come here?"

"Oh yeah. Not to... well, you know." She lifts her brows. "But just to see the place, walk through it. Make sure I hadn't moved anything. We'd sometimes have dinner together, but he'd never stay the night."

"Did he talk about any other houses he had like this? Secret places he liked to visit?" Anjelica asks.

Pippa studies her. "No, but Arne wasn't like that. I wasn't there to... to talk with him. I was there to listen, when we weren't doing a scene. He came to this house to tell me about Professor Hanult and how he believed in Arne and thought

Arne should be doing this and that, how Arne should be remaking the world. It wasn't anything like a relationship."

"And you were okay with that?" Anjelica asks.

Pippa gives a short laugh. "Okay? It was a job and a good one. I'll never have to work again thanks to what I've saved. Arne is the one you should feel sorry for. I was probably the person he was closest to after Minerva, and I can't say I miss him. I can go live my life now. What's he going to do?"

Ideally, he'll go to prison. But that doesn't seem likely. I don't say anything to Pippa though, because I don't know how much she knows about Fuchs's illegal activities.

"Did you and Minerva talk a lot?" Anjelica asks.

"No, not at all. She was his work wife—he kept all that very separate from me." Her smile goes cold. "He's probably hiding out with her somewhere. Does anyone know where she is?"

Anjelica and I very carefully do not look at each other since we know exactly where Minerva is. And she's not with Fuchs.

"She's in hiding too," I say, which is true. I make myself as blank as I possibly can. "So that's no help."

"Too bad." Pippa sinks back into her chair. "I wish I could help you since you helped me. If I see him, I'll call you. But I doubt he's coming back." Her mouth purses. "If you didn't know I was living here, how did you know to come by?"

"We have a listing of all the real estate owned by Corvus," Anjelica says smoothly. "This address stood out."

Pippa frowns. "He didn't own it personally?"

I shake my head. "Who knows why he did it that way, but he did."

"Probably to hide the fact that it meant something to him," Pippa says. "If it's held by some made-up company, no one can trace it to him. No one can use it against him."

I can't blame him for that. I used his relationship with

Pippa against him myself. For a good cause, but I still took advantage.

Guilt isn't what I'm feeling, because I don't regret what I did, but my chest is tight. I don't understand that, because I'm also glad I can give Pippa this house to repay her for what she did for me and everything she went through with Fuchs. It's confusing and I hate it.

"If you see him or hear from him or anyone else who might know where he is, would you call us?" Anjelica rises, signaling the end of the interview. "We really appreciate your talking to us, and I'm sorry we interrupted your evening."

"Yeah," I echo, because Anjelica said everything I wanted to.

Pippa hugs each of us in turn, which is surprising. She never struck me as a hugger before. "I was glad to help." She straightens up, juts out her jaw. "I'm going to sell the house once you sign it over to me. And the furniture. And then I'll be gone. I don't want him to find me again."

"Of course. If you need help disappearing…"

Pippa's smile is small but true. "I know where to find you."

Once we're back in the car, I don't drive off right away. I have to process what we heard, along with the hug. I didn't even think Pippa liked me, but she hugged me. The imprint of her arms around my shoulders still lingers. Not in the way Anjelica's kiss did on my mouth, but I can't shake this sensation either.

"You were looking for her?" Anjelica asks quietly.

What is Anjelica thinking? I could ask her, but I'm not sure I want to hear. There's disappointment in the slump of her shoulders, regret in the line of her mouth. For me, I'd bet.

"I was. It never occurred to me she'd be in a Corvus-owned house."

"You can't just have a company give her a house," Anjelica says. "Even if you do control the board."

Corporate governance? That can't be what she's really worried about. "I'm going to buy the house from Corvus, then give it to her."

Anjelica draws in a long breath through her nose, her chest rising. "What did she mean that you helped her?"

I don't hesitate to answer. Not with Anjelica—we're past that even if my subconscious twinges a hair in alarm. I ignore it. "She'd been planning to leave Fuchs for a while. She came to me to ask for help."

"Why you?" Her tone is as sharp and short as the words.

"I knew what was really going on between them."

"How did you figure that out?" She's relentless with these questions, jabbing me with them. The more I answer, the more she demands.

This time I take the long breath. She's not going to like this. "One of the employees at a start-up I invested in is cousins with Fuchs's pool guy. The pool guy wanted to expand his business—I gave him the funds and asked that he keep an eye out for anything unusual at Fuchs's house."

"He was spying on Fuchs for you?"

My mind rejects that word, hard. "The money I gave him was a loan," I say with deliberation, "which he's already paid back. I just mentioned that if he happened to see something, he could let me know. And he did. It wasn't much that he told me, a few touches between them that he saw. In the end, I confirmed it all with Pippa herself."

Anjelica faces me. Her eyes are wide, but the rest of her features are tight. "She told you what was going on?"

"I told you she was thinking about leaving. Pippa's not dumb—she wanted to keep all her cards on the table. And I was a good card to have."

Telling me wasn't some kind of confession or expression of trust, at least not in the usual definition of trust. Pippa and I were using the other as leverage. If she told Fuchs I had someone on his payroll in my debt, that I knew about their relationship, it would blow my entire plan to hell. I suppose I trusted Pippa as much as she trusted me in our strange relationship.

Anjelica watches me with what I think is sadness in her eyes. She lifts a hand, sets it against my cheek.

I gasp at the contact. Her hand is warm, her skin soft, and the touch of our skin is electric. I want to reach up, to hold her hand against me forever. But I stop myself. I shake inwardly from the effort, but I stop myself.

"You're full of contradictions, do you know that?" she asks. "Is there anyone out there who's done you a favor? Or do you always keep the balance on your side?"

"You." I turn my head so that her hand moves across my jaw. "You're helping me with this."

She watches me for a long moment. "So one person. That's it." She lets her hand fall. "And Mark, Logan, Finn, Paul, and Elliot. They count too."

"I made them all rich," I point out. "We are who we are because of the algorithm I developed."

It's perhaps the first time I've taken credit for it. Anjelica knows I wrote it—someone told her at some point, I'm not sure who—but I've never admitted it to anyone. No one knows besides the Bastards. And her.

She shakes her head. "The money is because of what you did. And the power. But who you all are… that came before. Money had nothing to do with it. Are you going to tell them about Pippa? The whole truth?"

"She wants to disappear. And I'm going to let her." I look up at the house, which is dark again. "Too bad she couldn't tell us more."

Anjelica looks too. "We did learn something very important," she says. "He goes back to places meaningful to him. And he wants them kept like he remembers. But he doesn't want anyone to know about those places."

She gives me a significant look. As if I too do that.

But I don't. I never revisit the past.

"Okay," I say. "So we just need to keep working our way through that list."

"Maybe." She taps her lip. "I think there's something we're missing though."

"What?"

"I don't know. He likes to hide things. I keep coming back to that." She sighs. "I'm going to be thinking about it all night."

"Then let's keep going through the list. Together." I'm not planning on sleeping much anyway. That list is going to be on my mind too.

Her gaze catches mine, holds. "At… at your place?"

I've never had her over to my house. Or anyone really. Occasionally I'll invite one of the Bastards over for a work meeting, but that's it.

She's asking to come in. Of course I can't say no to that.

"Sure." My voice is deeper than I expect. "My place it is."

CHAPTER 14

I asked him to take me to his house, to a place in his life I've never been... and he said yes.

Does he even realize he's opening up to me? Slowly, reluctantly, but it's happening. I never would have known about Pippa before. He'd have handled that entirely on his own, telling no one.

Maybe someday he can tell me all the other things he's done entirely on his own, kept secret from everyone else in his life. Maybe someday he can tell the rest of the Bastards too.

Maybe then I can rethink my rejection of him. Hell, I already am.

For right now I'll take this view from his apartment, which is stunning. He has two full floors at the top of one of the high-rises in SoMa, a penthouse to end all penthouses. There are views of the city from all sides, glittering beneath us like a living jewel. And here we are, surrounded by sleek luxury, sitting atop it all.

"Do you want anything?" Dev asks. "The housekeeper has the fridge stocked, although I'm not sure exactly what's in there."

"You don't know?" It's his fridge—shouldn't it be things he likes?

He shrugs. "She insists that I have some kind of food around even though I don't eat here much."

"Let's go see what's in the fridge then. We'll go through the list in the kitchen."

"Work in the kitchen?" He's genuinely confused, which looks adorable on him.

I'm about to tease him about doing homework at the kitchen table when I catch myself. He probably wasn't allowed to do things like that. When a kitchen is cooking for dozens and dozens of residents instead of a family, it probably isn't an informal gathering space.

"Where would you do your homework when you were a kid?" I ask instead as we head toward the kitchen.

"We were assigned desks," he says. "The school library was my favorite spot. It was quieter."

His kitchen is inhumanly clean. I'm guessing he's never once cooked in here. I'm wondering if he ever even learned to cook. But I'll save that question for another time.

When I open the fridge, I see his housekeeper has good taste. There are several really nice cheeses in there, some cured meats, fancy olives, and everything else you might want to throw yourself together a gorgeous snack. I start pulling things out, piling them on the island. A peek in the pantry reveals fresh french bread and even soft pretzels.

"We are going to have quite the feast," I tell Dev as I find the plates and silverware. "What happens to all this food when you don't eat it?"

"The housekeeper takes it home."

I pause with a plate in my hand. He's basically having his housekeeper buy groceries for herself with his money. I'm betting that was his idea somehow.

"Good for her." I set the plate in front of him and start

putting meat, cheese, bread, and fruit on it. "It's like a picnic indoors," I say when I finish.

He's wryly amused as he picks up a bite of pretzel with a smear of mustard on it. "I've never done this."

"Eaten in the kitchen?" I close my eyes as I swallow some gouda. Lovely. "Or had a picnic indoors?"

"Both."

I knew this kitchen was way too clean to have ever been used. Some deep itch in me wants to mess it up, to cook and eat and bring him into this room. The kitchen was always the center of our home growing up, where we did almost everything. My kitchen is probably my favorite room in my own house. I want him to have a favorite room, and I'm pretty sure he doesn't. The kitchen is a good place to start.

Dev's pulled out the listings and is already going through them. "Were there any foreign addresses that were conspicuous?"

"There're several there, but none that stood out like the Poland address." I lean over his shoulder so I can see what he's looking at. The scent of his soap—and his skin—surrounds me. If I tilt my head, I can kiss the patch of skin behind his ear, right between those two dark curls.

My fingers tingle as I remember him taking the pear from my hand, all the way back in Poland. How warm his mouth was, the soft caress of his tongue. How badly I wanted to offer him another one, my pulse hammering through every inch of me. Especially the inches between my thighs.

"I finished the pears," I blurt out suddenly. "I sent them back the jar along with some wine from Napa and lavender from the farmers' market. They sent me some plum jam. It's really good."

He turns his head and his eyes darken when he sees how close I am. "They gave you more fruit?" he asks slowly.

I nod.

"Is the jam as good as the pears?" His voice is so deep it

drags along my skin. I shiver even though he hasn't even touched me.

"No." I wet my lips. "Not quite."

For a moment I forget what we're even talking about. There's only the dark gold of his eyes, molten enough for me to drown in, his gorgeous skin, begging me to touch, and his lips…

I blink and straighten up. I came here to see his apartment and strategize about Fuchs. Dev might be opening up to me, but my initial objections about any kind of romantic relationship still stand. He's not ready. He can't just be candid with me—there are other people who care about him. He needs to see that.

Sleeping with him would scratch the deepest itch I've ever had, one I've been carrying for years. And it would open up even deeper wounds I suspect.

"Do you see anything interesting?" I ask in a slightly strangled voice.

He lets his gaze run from my head to my feet and back again, lazy and appreciative. But all he says is "Not yet."

I force myself to eat some more even though my stomach is jittery as all heck. "He really could be anywhere." I tear apart some bread. "We've learned something about where he's been but not where he'd be likely to go I guess."

"Mmm." Dev looks up at me through his lashes. "Are you having second thoughts?"

Am I? I slouch onto the stool, hooking a foot around the leg to steady myself. I don't think so. I'm just trying to fill the space between us with something other than attraction.

"No. We've seen part of his childhood, college… and his first and only job was running Corvus." Which leaves us at kind of a dead end because he's not…

Holy crap. I can't believe I didn't think of it. I snap upright, pushing the stool away. "What about his office?" I smack the countertop with my hand in a burst of excitement.

"That's where he spent most of his time. He's not there now, obviously, but what if he left some clue there?"

Why didn't I think of searching his office first? Probably because I was caught up in going through Fuchs's past before looking at his present.

Dev rubs his mouth. "I looked through it briefly when he first disappeared, but I didn't search it. What do you think he might have left?"

"We know he likes trophies. The pear tree, Hanult's house… he bought those to remind himself of victories. Was there anything like that in his office?"

Dev shakes his head. "Not that I saw. But you're much better at seeing those things than I am."

"You see things too. Just different ones than I do."

He makes a noise that might be disagreement. "We'll go through the office tomorrow together." He picks up the stack of addresses. "And mark any potential leads in these."

It takes about an hour, but eventually we get to the end. We check off any addresses that strike us as unusual, any places that aren't in cities with tech hubs, or anything else that catches our eye. We're not exactly being methodical since we don't really know what we're looking for.

The bread and the cheese disappear, and Dev opens a bottle of wine at some point. It's cozy, friendly… but beneath it all, our attraction lurks. As I laugh at one of his jokes, I can't help but notice the way his shirt pulls across his shoulders. Or when he reaches for a bite of food, the way the lines of his hands are strong, stark.

My body's awareness of him starts as a low background hum, then grows and grows until it's a hard buzzing in my ears. And from the way he keeps catching my gaze and holding it, those golden eyes hot, he feels the same buzz.

I resolved not to sleep with him, but with the heat between us and being in his house—finally he was opening up to me—that resolve was weakening.

When we got through the last page of addresses, I made myself straighten up and put on an impersonal smile. "Well, I'd better go. It's late and we have an office to search tomorrow."

He says nothing, merely watches me with that too-intent stare. It's not a mask this time—he knows exactly what he wants to do with me, and he's not hiding it.

I wet my lips. "I can't," I say softly. He's the most compelling man I've ever met... but he's still the most reserved too. I can't be the only person he trusts, the only one he ever opens up to.

He's got others who care about him and a lot of care in himself to spread around. I want him to see that, and I'm not sure he ever will even if he's confessed his past to me. It's a start, but it's not the end.

Immediately the mask is back in place. My whole body aches as he closes off again.

"I'll take you home."

We both move to pick up the plates and start cleaning up. As we do, it strikes me that the kitchen will be barren again once we're done. And when I'm gone, Dev will be all alone in this too-pristine, too-empty apartment.

It's what he wants, but it still hurts me to think about.

I reach for the fridge handle at the same time he does. Our forearms brush against each other, my bare skin on his. The heat of him is so shocking I pull back.

Too fast though, and I start to lose my balance. He grabs my elbow, steady, firm, and rights me. My pulse is loud in my ears, heavy between my legs. And breathing is like swimming through quicksand.

Dev releases me, and I see that his hand is shaking. He braces himself against the counter, his head dropping. Every inch of him is taut, steeled.

"Anjelica..." The torment in his voice tears at me. "I

can't… Being this close to you all the time… I can only hold back so much. You have to leave. Now."

I can't stop myself; I reach out for him. I know he's suffering because of me, because of what I asked him to do, but I can't help but try to comfort him.

But also because I'm as shaken as he is. My jaw is clenched at how badly I need to touch him.

When my hand makes contact with his back, everything in me unfurls. Like I can finally fill my lungs after years of being starved for oxygen.

He's so still under my hand he might have turned to stone. "Didn't you hear me?"

"I did. I… I don't know how far I can go, but I need at least some part of you."

I haven't been this vulnerable with a man since Kaleb. And I'm so, so terrified. But I can't ignore my need for Dev anymore.

He turns. Some of the torment seeps out of him. "Anjie." He cups my face, so gentle I want to cry. "Whatever you want, I'll give you." His thumb rubs over my cheek, and I turn in to his touch. "Let me touch you, please you. I swear I won't even take off my clothes. Just let me do… what I've been imagining."

His tone goes dark, velvety. He could ask me to do anything in that voice and I'd probably agree.

"And tomorrow? What happens tomorrow?" It was never going to be a one-night stand with us. Which is why I've tried so hard to avoid this. We're entangled, for better or worse, and this could make it much, much worse.

"I don't know." The honesty in that is open, real. "I don't know if I can be the man you want me to be. But… but I can say I'm not the man I was even a few weeks ago. I am trying."

"Oh." I close my eyes, bite my lip. When Dev goes raw, he goes heart-stoppingly raw. I open them again, and his gaze is molten. "This will complicate everything."

He actually smiles. "It was already complicated. And we'll go slow."

I know I can trust him, that my wants, my needs, will control everything he does. I'm more worried about my own heart, that it will fall for him without my permission. It might already be doing that.

But in the end, if he does break my heart, it won't be willingly. So I tilt my head and press a kiss into his palm, giving him permission to do what he's been imagining with me.

CHAPTER 15

Dev's bedroom is as stark as the rest of the apartment. Everything is done in sleek lines, luxurious materials, but the overall effect is impersonal. Like someone chose all this without really knowing him. His office is more personal, but that's probably because I decorated it for him.

It's too dark is what it is. Dev needs lightness around him.

But then he takes my arm, turns me to face him, and I forget about the decor. The heat in his eyes is all the light we'll need.

When he looks at me, his expression is completely open. He's drinking me in—no walls, no reserve, nothing between him and me.

It's heady, and I suddenly regret telling him I could only do so much. That I agreed to him keeping his clothes on.

But I'll regret it even more in the morning if I go back on our agreement. I have to protect something of myself, even as I give in.

I reach up, run my fingers through his hair. It's so thick and soft, the ends curling around my fingertips. If he let it grow longer, it'd be like a mane, a perfect frame for his golden eyes.

My hands begin to tremble as I imagine asking him to

grow his hair out, asking for anything from him beyond tonight.

Maybe someday I will. Maybe tonight is the first step toward something like that.

"Anjie?" He's felt my shiver; of course he has. There's never been anyone so attuned to me as he is.

"I'm fine." I smile, rake my fingers through his curls. "I've wanted to do this for a long time."

He doesn't smile back. He's intent, serious. Determined. When he reaches for the hem of my shirt, he goes slowly, waiting for me to stop him.

I don't want to stop him. I don't want it with an intensity that makes my muscles quake.

His fingers brush the waistband of my yoga pants as he gathers the first bit of my shirt hem. Then he takes another inch in his fist and he touches my bare skin.

A shudder runs through me, sweetly painful. Dev presses his palm against my stomach, steadying me. His hand is rock solid, his touch warm, electric.

I've literally dreamed about this moment. Hot, fevered dreams that I wake up from in a sweat.

This is a thousand times better than those dreams. Because he's real and he's touching my bare skin and the alarm isn't about to go off—I am.

He takes another inch of my shirt in his hand, lifts it until it's just under my rib cage. It's less than I'd show in a bikini, but his gaze makes me feel as if I'm entirely naked. So heated, so reverent, as if he's uncovering treasures. And it's only my stomach.

"Oh." He reaches out with his free hand and traces the line of one of my tattoos peeking out from under my shirt. "Can I see this?"

If tonight goes like we're planning, he'll see all my tattoos. But his asking to see this particular one—possibly the most innocent one I have in the most innocent place on me—does something strange to my heart. The same strange thing it often does with him.

"Yes." My voice is soft, thick with desire. I'm throbbing with achiness, and he's barely done anything.

He inhales with appreciative anticipation, tracing the lines that he can see. His every stroke is light, but they echo through me like an earthquake. When he finally pulls my shirt over my head and off, my thighs are shaking.

Once I'm shirtless, he sets a hand on either side of my ribs, framing me before him. He gives a low sigh of appreciation. "Wow."

The tattoo on my stomach is a tropical garden, lush and colorful, with birds of paradise bursting out of leaves of the deepest green. It's actually part of a larger piece that continues to my chest, but my bra cuts that off. The lines of the garden fade at the edges, the colors growing fainter and fainter until it's only black and white, so that the images seem to be rising out of a dark, bleak outline. Or dissolving back into it.

Dev strokes the leaves, the birds, the flowers, taking it all in with his hands. His fingers are long, strong, and his touch isn't light. He wants to know my skin.

I glance down, see his erection straining against his fly. My hand burns to stroke him, but I hold back. He said tonight was only about me and my pleasure, and I want to honor his request, the same as he's honored mine.

"You need to be on the bed for the rest of this." He gathers me up with muscular grace, my bare torso and shoulders tingling at the touch of him against me.

"I like that idea." I pull his head down to mine and kiss him. Light at first, one kiss, then another, lips to lips. It's like being tickled with a feather, quick but potent.

He lets me take the lead on the kissing, and I can feel his smile on my mouth, the pull of his lips, the slight tension there. He likes this.

So do I, but I want more. So I press my tongue to his lips, tasting him and asking for deeper. Oh, and he gives it to me. By the time we reach the bed, we're both panting, our mouths locked together. I've got a hard grip on his hair, and I'm so wet and hot I can feel it through my yoga pants.

With deliberate care, he lays me on the bed, his arms like steel, although he swallows hard once he's done.

"So beautiful," he whispers. He can't seem to stop touching my tattoos. "I never could have imagined this, not anything like this."

I stretch like a cat, beguiled by the notion that I'm beyond what even his brain could produce. He's got a very big brain, but I've managed to blow it.

He dips his head, and I brace myself for a kiss on my belly. Except not well enough, because I squeak when he *licks* me. Hot and soft and wet, a long, loving taste of my skin.

"Okay?" he asks without looking up. The amusement in his tone is a dark sparkle.

"Fine." I'm breathless, still squeaky, but I don't care. I want that tongue *everywhere* on me.

He obliges, tracing my tattoo with his mouth as thoroughly as he did with his hands. It raises me to a frantic fever pitch until I want to tear off the rest of my clothes, bare all of myself to him.

"Easy, easy," he murmurs between kisses. "We have time. So much time."

It doesn't feel that way. My body is running toward something big, something I've been chasing forever, and if I don't hurry, it will disappear. And no, it's not an orgasm. It's more than that.

"Please." I'm asking him to take me to that place or at least get the rest of my clothes off. My pussy needs attention, especially from his tongue. Now.

He helps me to sit up, then works off my sports bra. Somehow he manages to make even that a tease.

When he sees my chest, he gasps. Which is exactly the reaction I was hoping for.

Out of the jungle on my torso, a phoenix is bursting free, fiery heart inked right over mine, its wings of flame curled over my breasts. I got it after Kaleb's baby was born, made the appointment the day my mom sent me the birth announcement.

The baby was adorable, Kaleb and Harper looking so proud, so happy. So joyous. And I felt so angry, so abandoned, and also awful that I felt that way about a *baby. Some dark part of me wanted that to be my baby even though I knew by then I never would have been happy with Kaleb.*

I needed to mark myself but in a beautiful way. One that would remind me each and every time I saw it that I could move beyond pain to become something better.

Dev lifts his hand, his expression stunned. He wants to touch, but he's also hesitant. So I take his wrist, set his hand right on the heart of the phoenix. Beneath, my heart beats, hard and fast.

We breathe together as he holds me like that, his hand between my breasts. Anticipation builds in me until I'm trembling.

And then his fingers curl. A slight flex, a start, and his hands begin to move. He finds the lines of flame in the wings, the lines of me beneath, the curve of my breast, the jut of a nipple. His touch goes from learning to teasing, and I'm panting, jerking, almost out of my mind again.

"I can't even tell you how you look, how you feel," he says, voice rough with intent. "I don't know the words—they don't exist."

It's the same for the sensation building in me. It's past my words, almost past my mind. And he hasn't even touched me in the place I need him the most.

"I don't need words," I manage to say.

He smiles knowingly. And then he's reaching for the waistband of my pants.

I nearly sob with relief as I help him take them off, along with my panties. Being elegant or sexy or taking my time doesn't appeal at all—being completely bare to him does.

He arranges my legs so that I'm open, exposed, and the look on his face would kill any hesitation I have stone dead. He's… he's looking at me like I'm a wonder again. Although I suppose he's never really stopped.

"I love this." He traces the quote running around my leg. "What's it from?"

"Anaïs Nin." I gasp when he skims my curls. "She wrote some very dirty, very poetic stories."

"Mmm." He brushes my curls again, smiles when I gasp once more. Torments me in the sweetest way. "It's perfect. Every inch of you is a masterpiece."

Lord, he's getting me worked up with all this *perfection* and *masterpiece* talk. I've made my body into a canvas, and having him appreciate it so deeply is almost as lust inducing as his hands on me.

He lowers his mouth to my pussy and shows me real lust then. He licks and kisses and makes deep noises of satisfaction like he's feeding a desperate hunger in himself.

I'm so close to the edge it doesn't take much of his talented mouth—or those noises—to have me at the peak of my climax. It's so close—building, building, building, until I think I can't take another moment or I'll shatter. And then it keeps going.

"Dev." I'm begging him to help, to give me what he promised.

With two thick fingers, he slips inside me, stroking my core, his mouth licking and sucking. And then I'm caught by it, my entire body clenching in the most exquisite way, unraveling into wave after wave of pleasure.

He gentles his touch, stays with me as I come back down.

I'm limp, wrung out, covered with a fine sheen of sweat. I can't remember the last time an orgasm went through me like that. Probably never.

Gathering me close, he tucks us both beneath the covers. He's still wearing his clothes, which makes me frown.

"You should change," I mumble. I can feel his erection pressing into my hip, thick and hard, but I don't reach for it. He wanted to give me this, entirely free and clear of his own pleasure. And I'll let him. This time.

I don't think too hard on what that means for us, that there will be a next time. Something to wrestle with tomorrow.

"I will. In a second."

He doesn't suggest I take a shower, call for a car, go home. He's invited me inside and he's not kicking me out.

So I decide to stay.

CHAPTER 16

I want to touch Anjelica again. I'm desperate to touch her again.

But I don't. She's sleeping, and while she agreed last night to let me touch her—God, did she agree, full throatedly—we haven't discussed anything in the cold light of day.

I almost don't want her to wake up, because then she'll leave. But I can't lock her up or ask her to do anything she doesn't completely want to. I don't want her to stay out of pity.

Watching her like this is even skirting a line. I can't help it though—she's so beautiful and she's in my bed. I'd dare anyone to look away from a dream come true.

Eventually though I get up and order in some breakfast. I know her favorite is lox and a bagel, heavy on the capers, hold the onions, which I call in to a café around the corner. I order some coffee too, the kind we get at Bastard Capital, which is also her favorite. I know because she's the one who orders it for us. I think we wouldn't even notice if she gave us instant coffee crystals, but she always goes above and beyond.

When I come back, she's still sleeping. So I duck into the

bathroom, shower, shave, and dress for the day. The entire time, I'm very aware of her on the other side of the door, so aware my half erection never subsides. Today is going to be a long day if this keeps up. I used to be better at managing my reaction to her, but the floodgates are open now.

She's awake when I come out, sitting up with the sheet tucked around her even though she put on one of my T-shirts last night. Her expression is shy and creased with sleep. Her amazing hair is the most glorious tangle—she'd probably scream if she could see it, but I'm loving it. It makes me think of spending all day in bed with her.

"Sleep okay?" I'm not quite sure how this morning should go or how she wants it to go, but that seems safe.

She nods. "Did you? I kind of took over your bed."

"There's plenty of space." I run a hand through my wet hair. "I ordered breakfast. Your favorite."

Anjelica smiles as she ducks her head. "Thanks. I'll be down in a minute."

So that's how she wants the morning to go—no more intimacy, at least not the physical kind. But we can smile and speak without awkwardness.

I'm happy with that.

I leave her to get ready. The breakfast arrives, and I set it out on the dishes I hardly ever use. I debate putting it in the dining room, but I decide on the kitchen in the end. Anjelica seemed to like this room last night.

When she comes down, I've already got my laptop open, working through my messages on Slack.

"Morning," she says briskly. Her hair is wet, hanging in loose curls around her face, and she's wearing her clothes from yesterday. "Why are you frowning?"

"I should have washed your clothes. Or ordered new ones." Stupid of me not to think of it, but the morning-after logistics haven't been something I've dealt with in a while. A long time actually. Years, in fact.

She rolls her eyes affectionately. "Do you know how to wash clothes?"

My breath hitches. "I've been washing my own clothes since I was nine," I say softly.

Her face falls. "Right. I should have remembered."

"No," I say, "you shouldn't have. I should have told you."

She reaches for my hand. "You just did."

Her smile makes me want to slay dragons, move mountains, bring back whatever treasure she asks for. I wish I could think of more of my secrets to give her, just to keep seeing that smile. But I think she has them all.

When she pulls back her hand, I let myself feel the loss. Just this once.

"You really did get my favorite," she says as she takes in her breakfast. "And there're no onions." She takes a sip of coffee. "Mmm, that's good."

I salute her with my own cup. "It's nothing."

"I'm going to disagree." She piles her bagel high with lox and tomatoes and capers. "What's on the agenda today? An office break-in?"

"Yes, but we don't *have* to break in. Minerva told me how to get in to Fuchs's office. Unless there's a hidden part she can't access, we should be good."

"There's definitely a hidden part we can't access," she says. "Remember who we're talking about. So how do we get into that?"

The most obvious answer is Finn, but he's not too happy with me at the moment. He's never before said no when I've asked him for help, but that streak might be broken if I ask him now.

"Minerva might be able to crack any locks."

Anjelica gives me a look because she knows Finn is the logical choice too. And she's disappointed I didn't suggest it. "Let's see what we find. Maybe he's made it easy for us."

She starts to laugh at her own joke, and I have to join in.

Because of course it won't be easy and because her laugh is infectious. There's nothing snarky or mean about her laugh —she loves life and people, and it shows.

We finish our breakfast in an easy quiet. I've got a million things to deal with at work and so does she—she's scrolling through her phone, typing out replies with her thumbs. She's incredibly quick with that tiny phone keyboard.

"How's your company looking?" I ask. "The one you were talking about at the partners' meeting?"

Her eyes light up. "Oh, I hope really well. I just love the founder so much. Her vision for the app is so…" She sighs. "She believes in it so hard. I want to make it happen for her. We've got a meeting this morning actually."

I hold back the words of caution I want to give her. Anjelica already knows that she should maintain some distance, to not *love* the founders you invest in. You need a clear head at all times and to know when to pull the plug. If you love something, you're not going to be able to make the tough choices.

It's the founder's dream, not Anjelica's. She doesn't have to take on that burden.

But I'd only be repeating things Anjelica's aware of. Still, her excitement makes me uneasy. I don't want her to be hurt if this company goes under. Or if the next one does, or the one after that. The failure rate in the tech world is much, much higher than the success rate, even for Bastard Capital.

"I hope it goes well" is all I say. "Do you want to go to Corvus in the afternoon then?"

She taps at her phone screen. "I can have Georgia reschedule my afternoon, yeah. And jeez, look at the time. I —" She catches my eye, takes a deep breath.

She's preparing her farewell. I can see it, the uncertainty in her expression. She's not sure how to do this. I'm not sure myself.

"I'll call up the car," I say, saving her from trying to find the right words. "And…"

Now I'm lost. Thank you would be all wrong, and while I really, really hope we do this again, I'm not going to pressure her. And I already know I'll see her soon.

She bites her lip, hesitating, then leans over and kisses me. It's not exactly chaste—she puts too much tongue in it for that, thank God—but it's not leading anywhere. It's a kiss for a kiss's sake, the mood of the morning perfectly caught in it.

When she pulls back, I find something to say. "I'll miss you."

She touches my jaw. "But I'll see you soon."

And those are the right words. We found them.

I walk her down to the waiting car, help her inside. I watch it until it disappears, then wait a moment more. We definitely crossed some kind of bridge last night, but I'm not certain where exactly we've arrived. And I don't have the time to sit around and ponder it.

When I get back to my apartment, I open my laptop. And stare at it.

I know what I need to do. Anjelica does too. So why aren't I doing it?

Being at odds with my partners wasn't supposed to upset me. I said it didn't, and I wasn't lying. Before, I would have called up Finn even if he was angry at me. Because I wouldn't care, or at least I'd tell myself I don't.

But I do. I don't want to call him, to face the awkwardness between us. The thought is making me feel… bad. Anjelica wants me to feel bad so that I'll fix it, but I don't like this. This is what I've tried to avoid.

Clenching my jaw, I grab my phone. He's probably asleep and won't even answer.

Only he does. On the second ring.

"What?" That's how he answers, and it bristles.

Fuck, I've got to say something, and nothing's coming to mind. All I want to do is tell him I need help, but I sense that would be wrong.

Correction, I know it's wrong. I need to break the ice between us, even just a crack.

"I'm surprised you're awake." There, that's a decent start.

"Gonna just leave a voice mail?" Finn says dryly. "You know I don't listen to those." There's a rasping sound, like he's rubbing his beard. "Doc got up early to go for a run."

So he woke up too, and he's waiting for her to get back. Probably fighting the impulse to go after her and make sure she's okay. Doc can more than take care of herself, but Finn likes taking care of her too.

"You didn't go with her?"

"Umm…" He clears his throat. "She, uh, asked me not to go with her because we kind of turned it into a competition the last time we ran together."

I can imagine—those two have elevated fighting into foreplay. "Couples run didn't go so well, huh?"

"There might have been puking at the end."

I laugh because it's so typical of them. "You or her?"

"Me," he says sheepishly.

That sounds typical too. "That… is exactly what I expected."

There's a beat where we're almost back to how things used to be. For a moment. And then the silence hangs too long and we're awkward and strained again.

"What do you need?" Finn asks briskly.

"I'm going through Fuchs's office again today. He's got to have stuff hidden in there, locked up nice and tight. I wanted to ask you what I might expect to find. Since you've snuck in there once before."

Finn isn't exactly vain, but he is justifiably proud of his

hacking skills. And his trip into Corvus was pretty damn amazing.

"Unless he went completely off the rails for the security in his office," Finn says, "it's probably the same shit he was using to lock up the rest of Corvus. I can send you the specs of what I saw and loan you some of my equipment. Minerva didn't have a complete map of all his hidey-holes for you?"

"There was some stuff he kept even from her. I figure it can't hurt to go through his office again."

"What are you looking for in there? Because you're searching for something."

My jaw clamps shut. How the hell did Finn figure that out? It's none of his business what I'm doing.

Slowly I force the muscles in my face to release. Of course Finn had to suspect something was up. I've asked him and Minerva about getting into hidden files within Corvus—my interest is too deep to be casual.

"I think Fuchs has something… something from my childhood." I'm not ready to give him any more than that.

"Oh." It's all Finn says for a while. And I'm not planning on saying anything else. "Well, if you need help cracking encryption or whatever on any files you find, let me know."

His offer is stiff, a touch hesitant. Not like how Finn would have offered before. But he did offer.

"Thanks." I put my very real gratitude into that. "For all your help. I hope one day I can tell you everything behind this."

Anjelica would be so pleased. I've made a move, offered some of my rationale and even my past to Finn. This is what she said she wanted.

"Me too." Finn doesn't sound as satisfied as I expected. "When are you going to let Doc into those archives to find all the files on her brother?"

I picture Doc going through the archives, finding my birth records before I can, sharing them with Finn, the two of them knowing my parents first. Or worse, Doc seeing them and passing them by, not knowing what they are. The records might remain buried, so close to discovery, just hiding in plain sight for who knows how much longer.

No. I don't want her in there. Or Finn or anyone else. I have to be the first. I have to find it, and then they can go wild in there. But the first discovery is mine.

"Minerva gave her all the records already." My tone is flat. Blank.

"We don't know that it was all of them. Not even Minerva knows that." Finn's voice is rising into true anger. "Seriously, what the fuck is your problem? What are you hiding in those archives?"

"Nothing." The bite in my voice surprises me. "I'm not hiding anything. I'm looking for it."

"What is it then?"

Why can't I just tell him? What the hell is wrong with me that I have to be so damn secretive?

Because even when the people surrounding me are showing they can be trusted, have been doing it for years, I still can't believe it. I'm... blocked. Like, fundamentally blocked, wrong compared to the rest of them. Anjelica seems to think I can magically be different, but she doesn't understand.

I exhale. "I'm not ready to say what it is. But when I find it, Doc is free to search the archives. I can promise that."

Even giving Finn that much is making my jaw clench, my fists curl. But I did it.

When Finn speaks again, he's resigned. Like he's starting to give up on me. "Okay, man. I'll bring that stuff for you into work today."

I want to tell him wait, that I can tell him more. And then just tell him everything. From being left at the fire station all the way to yesterday when Anjelica and I finally reconnected. Really, truly reconnected.

But I don't, because I can't unlearn a lifetime of instincts in a few seconds.

"Thanks. I'll see you there."

I hang up and wonder what Anjelica would have made of all that.

CHAPTER 17

This meeting with Helen isn't going as well as my first one. In fact, it's awful.

I sigh, look at the numbers she's given me again. "I'm sorry, but the subscriber numbers are going down? Like, the actual *number* of subscribers?"

After all the rosy growth projections Helen has given me, the user base is shrinking. People are canceling their subscriptions—and more people aren't signing up fast enough to make up the loss.

This is very bad. This looks fatal for Helen's company. *My* company too, since I'm an investor.

"We couldn't push the update we promised," she says. "And the marketing isn't... It's just not working."

"The marketing person has no idea why it's not?"

Helen shakes her hanging head. "No. I don't know enough about it to help her, and I don't know how it's going wrong."

My first instinct is to comfort her, tell her everything will be okay. That I'll make everything okay.

But I'm not her fairy godmother. I can't grant her wishes —I need to give her some tough love.

"This is bad." I look her straight in the eye. "Very bad."

Helen purses her mouth. "I know. But I don't want to fire my head of marketing. She's so nice."

I don't want her to fire the woman either. But a subscription app without subscribers isn't going to survive.

"Let's bring in a consultant to look at what's going on, give some suggestions," I say. "But if things don't turn around, she'll have to go."

Helen nods in relief.

"Now, let's talk about the missed update," I say. "And the falling subscriber numbers."

Helen's relief vanishes. "That was all my fault. I pushed the developers to get the update out, hyped it to the subscribers, promised it by a certain date, but it had a bug in it. A major one. I didn't let them do enough testing, then I pushed the update... and the app crashed. Completely."

The blood drains out of my face as she tells me that. When she's done, my cheeks are cold. "And then people started canceling."

Helen swallows hard. "Yes. But I reverted back to the old version as soon as we found out."

Not before she pissed off enough subscribers for them to cancel. "So the app broke and there's still no update. What do the reviews on the app store look like now?"

"Bad," Helen says faintly.

The entire situation is more than bad, but she already realizes that.

"That update needs to be out. Immediately. And it needs to be so amazing it knocks the current subscribers' socks off. So amazing even nonsubscribers are blown away."

Helen licks her lips. "Right. I completely understand."

She slinks out of my office, her shoulders slumped. I feel like the wicked witch, but it had to be done. If things don't turn around and fast, Helen's dreams will go up in flames.

Still, I wish I didn't have to be the bad guy. I prop my chin in my hand and ponder my orchids, trying to find a calm center. I need to do some clipping in there—I just haven't had the time, between becoming partner and helping Dev.

Dev. I let my head tilt to the side and my mouth stretch in a dreamy smile. Last night was amazing. He did exactly what he promised—blew me apart with pleasure and put me all back together again, without even taking off his clothes.

I shouldn't be imagining what it might be like if he did take his clothes off. I know that would be dangerous—my heart wouldn't survive it. I'd fall completely for him then and he's… he's still so alone.

My smile dies. If I fall for him, give in completely to what's between us, I worry that I'll always be the only person he has. The only one he ever lets in.

Finding his parents' identity might help. He might finally be able to see past his childhood then. But even if he could see past it, would that be enough to make him imagine a bigger future? One involving more than just me and him, together? Because we can't be a bubble of just two.

I don't know. I just don't know. It felt so right last night, but when I consider everything, there's still so much to overcome with him. I can't puzzle my way out of it.

There's a quiet knock at the door. Without even turning, I know it's Dev—that's how he knocks at my door. My body immediately lights up even before I've seen him.

And when I do see him leaning in the doorway, wearing a shirt that outlines his lean muscles, his soft jeans hugging his hips and thighs, my body goes incendiary.

"Hey," I say, breathless as a teenager seeing her crush.

He smiles kind of shyly, and it's like a roundhouse kick to my heart. He had me screaming his name last night with that mouth and he smiles like that? Gah.

"Hey." His voice is deep and scratchy and makes my toes curl.

We simply look at each other, him smiling like that and

me probably looking starstruck. What happened last night hangs between us, light and bouncy as a balloon.

"Are you ready?" he asks.

My mood drops some. We're going to search Fuchs's office today, and I don't like the idea of what we might find. He collected secrets, dirty ones—I'm not expecting to find anything I want to see.

Dev, however, has an energy in him—a touch anxious but also excited. He must be hoping he'll find something about his parents.

I want to be excited for him, but I can't help my unease. I just can't shake the feeling that even if he finds what he's looking for, it won't be enough.

"Yep" is all I say though. I grab my purse and we're off.

The Corvus building is the creepiest office space in Silicon Valley. Maybe even the entire world. The security guards at the front desk look a little nicer now, but they still have to buzz us in because there are no handles on the doors. Any of them.

In the hallways, people have put up printed signs to show where things are. And they've gotten creative with it—a break room has been renamed the Feasting Hall, and the name they've given the bathroom makes me blush.

Dev has a pass card that lets him in all the doors, the locks clicking open at his merest approach. The entire building seems to bend to him. As the employees pass by us, they make eye contact and nod to him. There's a palpable sense of relief in them as they do. Like people waking up from an awful nightmare.

Once we're in the elevator to the floor with Fuchs's office —yes, he took an entire floor for himself—I turn to Dev. "Do they know you're shuttering the company?"

"I've told them." He's wearing his impassive mask again. "I've also brought in an entire team to help them look for new jobs. And I've promised that no one will be let go for at least another year."

I suppose that's fair. "They look at you... It's interesting how they look at you. Like you've rescued them even though you're shutting them down."

His reserve cracks a hair. "I'm not Fuchs. That's why they look at me like that. They're not as afraid of me."

He's tearing apart their company and putting them out of a job, and they're not as afraid of him as their old boss. Which is pretty damning for Fuchs.

The elevator comes to a stop, but the doors don't open. And don't open.

My heart slams against my ribs. I don't like this. Not at all.

Then Dev reaches forward and presses his thumb against a pad. A light comes on and scans his face. Finally the doors slide open.

I suck in a deep breath as I rush through them. "Oh God, I thought we were stuck."

Dev follows behind me, calm as ever. "No, just Fuchs's insane security measures. Minerva was the only employee ever allowed up here."

"Not even the janitor crew?"

He shakes his head. "Minerva had to clean it."

I can't say that I like Minerva even though Elliot loves her and she makes him happy, but hearing that makes me feel for her. She really was in Fuchs's thrall. Or pretending to be.

There's a short hallway—nothing in it—and another set of doors. No knobs on those either.

"You're kidding me," I say.

Dev's got a wry expression on his face as he walks up. He puts his hand on a palm scanner and lets yet another console scan his face. "What, you think this is too much?"

"Clearly Fuchs didn't."

The door swings open silently, eerily. I'm half expecting a mummy or a ghost to pop out. But nothing does.

I take two careful steps inside. It's a massive open space with enclosed glass cases like you'd find in a museum. The cases are filled with sleek ceramic sculptures done in whites and grays and blacks without any defining features. They've all been smoothed into blankness.

"I'm told the pieces are very valuable," Dev says. "I don't know anything about art."

They look expensive. And cold. I get the sense that was the artist's idea, to make me feel unsettled when I look at them.

At the end of the room is a desk. There's nothing on it and nothing under it. It's simply a sheet of glass held up by four thin legs. No drawers, no computer, no pens, no paper.

Now *this* is an impersonal space. Dev's bedroom is bursting with personality compared to this.

"Did he make it this creepy on purpose?" I ask.

Dev is messing with some kind of console on the wall. He's got a duffel bag open at his feet, with electronics peeping out of it. "Maybe. He probably thought it looked cool and had the added benefit of freaking people out. Not that anyone else saw it."

"What did Minerva say about it?"

"She only told me how to open everything—she didn't give an opinion."

No, she wouldn't. In her own way, Minerva is as close-mouthed as Dev. I read the plaques under each sculpture, listing the artist's name—Kee Grantland—the year they were made, and the name of the piece. The names are deeply weird, like they were pulled from a random word generator. *Bucket Awful* and *Exclude Receipts* are some of the more normal ones.

I feel like I'm missing something with the sculptures. Like Fuchs has hidden some meaning within them that I'm *this* close to grasping. He's not an art guy, so why these? Yes, they're creepy and valuable, but...

I squint at one of the... forms, a cylinder of deep, gleaming black. If there's a deeper meaning in the art, I'm not seeing it. But what would Fuchs see when he looked at these? Because he was the only one who did once the pieces were here.

Or maybe I'm searching too hard for a meaning. Maybe there is none.

Dev makes a small noise of triumph, pulling me out of my thoughts. He steps back from the console, which is lit up.

Light suddenly pours onto each of the sculptures. Somehow they look even stranger with light bouncing off the polished surfaces, banging into the odd angles of them.

Dev points to one of them. "I want to get this case open."

So he feels there's more to the sculptures too. I look at the case nearest me, a square of impenetrable plexiglass. There's no opening I can see. I could try to lift it off, but I won't be able to raise it high enough to clear the sculpture.

"Is there a way in?"

Dev is studying his case. "That's what I'm trying to figure out."

"What do you think is inside?"

"Maybe nothing." But the way he's looking at that case, I don't think he believes that.

I suddenly want so badly for him to find what he's searching for. After last night I want... I want him. But he needs to get closure on this before he can move forward with anything. With me or with the Bastards.

I resist the urge to cross my fingers as he examines the case from all sides, putting a hand on one corner. I'm not sure what he's looking for since it looks very solid and seamless to me.

"Hmm." He steps back. "I wonder if this will work."

He goes back to the console in the wall and pulls some

electronics from the duffel bag. I'm not sure what he's doing —he plugs the electronics into the console, and numbers pop up on the screen of the electronic thingy. And that's about the extent of my knowledge about whatever's happening.

It seems to take forever, although it can't be more than a minute. I'm holding my breath instead of crossing my fingers, waiting for something to happen for him.

There's a whoosh of air from all the cases, which makes me jump. "What the heck?"

Dev doesn't react. He acts like he was expecting it.

With a slow lurch, the cases rise in the air, propelled by small legs that were hidden inside the bases.

"Oh." I put my hand over my mouth. I never expected something like this. I reach for the sculpture nearest me and pick it up.

Immediately an alarm starts to blare. I put the sculpture back as quick as I can, my heart pounding. The alarm keeps going.

"Shit," I hiss.

Dev is laughing, almost doubled over with it. "What did you think would happen?"

I don't think it's *that* funny. "So he never even picked them up once they were open? He's the only person up here! Even when it's just him, he can't let anyone touch his stuff. He's pathological."

"He is." Dev does some things to the console, and the alarm cuts out. "But if he's alarmed these beyond putting them in the cases, there might be something else there." He nods to the sculpture. "Try again."

"Is it going to scream at me?"

"I don't think so."

I'm not encouraged by that or by the thought that Fuchs might have put more than an alarm on these—like booby traps and blow darts. But I wrap my hand around the sculpture anyway. Slowly, with my breath held, I lift it.

The alarms stay silent. My shoulders sag with relief. But not too far—the sculpture is heavy.

I carry it to the desk. The sculpture makes a deep thunk when the base hits the glass of the desk. Dev comes over to join me.

"What are you looking for?"

"We're looking for… I'm not sure what." He runs his hand down the side of the sculpture, his skin stark against the deep black of the surface.

"Will we need to break it?" I'm suddenly afraid for these pieces. They're not to my taste, but I don't want to destroy them.

He knocks on it with his knuckles. It makes a hard, full sound—there's no empty space inside this thing. "I don't think so. Fuchs would do something more elegant to hide things—and every time he has something he wants to add to his stash, he breaks the sculpture open and has to get a new one made?" Dev shakes his head. "Not likely. And like I said, the sculptures are valuable. The artist doesn't create anymore."

"What?"

"Fuchs commissioned these pieces, and as part of the contract, she could never make a work of art for sale purposes again. He not only wanted to own these sculptures, he wanted to make sure no one else could own her work."

A cold lump forms in my stomach. "She was okay with that?"

"I don't know about okay. She was paid a lot, and she can still make items for personal reasons—she just can't sell them. Or give them away, although she could probably challenge that in court. But she hasn't."

"You talked to her." Of course Dev researched this artist, found every bit of information he could. Set up some favors so she would owe him.

He shakes his head. "She refused to see me. And I couldn't

get to anyone close to her. But Fuchs's legal team had to tell me everything when I took over Corvus."

Even though Dev was thwarted, I'm pleased about that. It's a good lesson for him, to not always get what he wants when he does these things. He might have amassed a ton of power in Silicon Valley with his manipulations, but he's taken down one of the tech world's biggest, baddest companies already—he can slow down now. He doesn't have to keep collecting other people's secrets.

"Well, I hope she's at least happy." I run one finger down a corner of the sculpture. "That's a lot to give up."

Dev leans back, done with his examination. I'm not sure what he was looking for, but he looks a touch satisfied, so he must have found something. "I tore up the contract. Released her from it."

"You… you can do that? Fuchs didn't personally make the contract with her?"

One corner of his mouth quirks up. "No, the contract was technically with Corvus. Because corporations are much more powerful than people when it comes to the law."

There's a rush of warmth in my chest, a stinging burst behind my eyelids. He broke the contract. He gave the artist her passion back.

Sometimes he can take my breath away. And those are the best times.

"Thank you," I say huskily. "For her sake."

He inclines his head in response. "I'm giving all these pieces back to her when we're done. She can sell them, smash them, do whatever she wants with them."

"It's a good plan. But how will we know when we're done with them?"

He picks up the sculpture. "We'll know when we know."

We go through the rest of the artwork, picking each piece up, examining it, looking for anything out of the ordinary, any clue that might be there. Handling them doesn't make them any less unnerving, with their cold, slick surfaces and shapes that refuse to coalesce into anything meaningful.

They also don't seem to be hiding anything. We get through ten of them, all without any luck.

"There's only two left," I say as we set another one back. "Are we sure we'll find something? These might not mean anything at all to Fuchs."

Dev releases his end of the sculpture with a grunt. "He wouldn't have basically ended the artist's career if they didn't mean something to them. Just because we don't see the meaning doesn't mean it's not there. He's hidden something somewhere. I know it."

I'm not so convinced. And I'm wondering if Dev is allowing his desperation to find his parents to cloud his better sense.

But there's only two left, like I said. It can't hurt to keep looking.

It will hurt Dev if we don't find anything though.

We move to the next one, which is the largest. It's a sort of sickly, pale green, a color that makes me think of stomach upsets. The curves of it fold in on themselves, like it's about to collapse. And it looks very, very heavy.

I really, really don't want to touch this one. But there's no choice.

Dev takes one corner, or at least the closest thing to a corner the piece has, and I take the other.

"One, two, three." Dev counts off and on three, we lift.

My arms strain from the load, my breath blowing out with the effort. It's even heavier than I thought.

"Okay?" Dev's straining too. I can tell from his tone.

"Yeah." I grunt that out. "Let's move."

We take two steps, maneuvering it carefully off the base. I squeal when the sculpture clears the pedestal.

"There, look!" I resist the instinct to drop the piece and

grab the thin sliver of something on the base. Something that wasn't on the others.

"Hang on. Take it to the desk."

We sidestep as quick as we can to the desk, setting the piece down way less gently than we did the others. And then we race back to the pedestal.

The sliver of something is a USB key. Small, unassuming, the kind you can pick up at the grocery store these days. We both stare at it as if it's something bigger, more explosive.

"Is that it?"

"I think so." Dev doesn't reach for it though.

So I grab it. It's barely bigger than a key in my palm. But it's probably got some of the most explosive secrets in the tech world on it.

"How did Fuchs manage to move that thing by himself?" I doubt he had Minerva help him.

Dev merely shrugs in response. He seems to have forgotten all about the artwork.

"Did you bring a laptop?" I ask.

Dev still looks stunned, like he can't believe we really found something. Which is odd given his earlier assurance that we would.

He blinks like I've woken him up. "Um, no. We can't just plug it into any machine. There was a dead man's switch on the files Finn took out of Corvus. I bet there's one on there too."

That makes sense. If Fuchs went to all this trouble to hide the drive, he'd probably put a booby trap on the drive itself. If the wrong person opens the drive, the dead man's switch will erase all the files.

"So what do we do?" I hold up the drive between my forefinger and thumb.

Dev stares at it. "We take it to the secure facility. Finn and Doc are already waiting."

I want to ask him if told Finn what he was looking for here, what he expected to find. I hope so.

But that's also between him and Finn. And I'm also desperate to see what's on this drive, if it holds what Dev needs. So I don't.

"Let's go then" is all I say. The rest can wait.

CHAPTER 18

Finn and Doc were already waiting when we arrived at the secure facility. And when I told them we pulled the USB drive out of a hiding spot in Fuchs's office, they didn't ask any more questions—they immediately got to work.

I wouldn't have been able to answer them anyway. I've hardly been able to breathe since we found it.

My parents are so close. I can feel it.

Finn is on video chat with Minerva, the two of them speaking in low voices as Finn types into a command window. I can catch snatches of their conversation: "Maybe that might work... Nope, try... Oh, we're getting..."

Anjelica and Doc are sitting together, talking about Doc's brother. Doc's been working on getting his conviction overturned with Finn's help. And Elliot's, although probably less now that he and Minerva are in hiding.

"It's just such a slog," Doc is saying. "For every step forward we take, there's two back. And the waiting... The judge just keeps pushing back the dates as if this isn't about a real, living being, only a pile of paperwork."

The sympathy in Anjelica's expression is radiant. It makes my chest ache, how deeply she feels for Doc and her brother. There might even be tears shining in her eyes, although she makes encouraging noises to Doc. *I hear you. I share your pain. Your tempered hope.*

People love Anjelica because she feels their hopes and sorrows as deeply as they do. I can't even imagine what that's like, to take on other people's emotions along with your own. Doesn't it hurt? Doesn't it weigh on her?

Maybe that's why I need her. She can feel the things for me I can't anymore. But she seems convinced I can, if I just try.

Maybe whatever is on this USB drive will let me do that.

"Yes!" Finn pounds his fists on the table. "We're in."

We crowd around his monitor. On the video chat, Elliot pokes his head next to Minerva. She turns to smile at him, her expression absolutely glowing. And Elliot... *glows* back. I never thought either of them could ever look like that.

I don't wear that expression when I look at Anjelica. But I understand it.

"What's in there?" Anjelica asks Finn.

"Yeah, what is it?" Doc leans over his shoulder, wrapping her arms around him.

"It's us," he says.

And sure enough, there are folders labeled with our names—all the Bastards and Anjelica. There's one for Callie, one for Doc, and even one for Grace. Minerva's not there, but that's because this must have been made before she escaped Corvus. Fuchs must have trusted her until the very end.

No one moves as we look at the screen. That folder with my name on it could have everything I've ever been looking for. My entire identity, just a click away.

But everyone is watching. I can handle Anjelica seeing what's inside there, but others... A cold sweat breaks out on my skin.

"You've got a file here," Finn says to Elliot. "But Emily, you don't."

The relief on Emily's face is clear even through the spotty video link. "Thanks," she says. She and Elliot share a look. "We'll hang up now, but can you send us Elliot's file?"

"Sure thing." Finn calls up a command window, sends off the files. "Done. Thanks for your help."

No one asks me if the files should be sent. I suppose my bringing it to Finn has made it communal property, not that I really object. Just as long as no one sees what's in my folder.

Once they're gone, we go back to staring at the files. I've never wanted to open something more, and I've never wanted to be alone more. I can't wait to see what's there, but I'd rather peel my skin off than show that to Finn or Doc.

"Open mine," Doc says.

"You sure, babe?" Finn looks over his shoulder at her.

"Yeah." She reaches for the mouse, clicks on the files. "I've got nothing to hide."

In the end, she's right. There's a lot about her brother and the panopticon program and her involvement in the protests against it, but nothing we didn't know. Nothing to be ashamed of.

Finn watches her carefully as she looks through the files. "You okay?" he asks when she closes the last one.

"Yeah." Her voice is quiet. "I'd guessed that he knew it was my brother he put in prison, but seeing it... I'm okay." She squeezes him once. "Now do yours."

"Oh shit." Finn sighs. "Mine's gonna be way worse."

Except it isn't. It's mostly about the public works Finn has financed in his hometown.

"You..." Anjelica points to a photo of a massive sports complex that Finn gave money for. "You've rebuilt an entire town."

Finn looks like a kid called to the principal's office, except with tattoos and a beard. "No. That's..." He shifts uncomfortably.

"He doesn't like anybody to know that he's not always a

hacker bad boy," Doc stage-whispers to Anjelica. "He doesn't want to ruin his rep."

I already knew most of this about Finn—he told me bits and pieces and I put it all together—but I understand the impulse to hide it. Even if it is something that can only make him look good.

Anjelica laughs, then slowly her expression freezes. "We probably shouldn't look at anyone else's files if they're not here. It wouldn't be right."

"Yeah," Finn says slowly. "We should send them the files unopened."

There's a heavy pause. Finn and Doc opened theirs… but Anjelica and I haven't. Finn and Doc aren't going to force us to, but there's still the imbalance there.

"Open mine." Anjelica's voice is firm. Determined.

"You don't—" I stop when she pins me with a defiant look.

"I'm not afraid."

I don't know if she means I shouldn't be either. *Afraid* isn't the right word for how I feel. It's much deeper and darker than that. It's a lifetime of wanting and waiting building in me. Not fear.

"Here." Finn gets up, offering his chair to Anjelica. "We can…" A look passes between him and Doc.

Anjelica takes the chair, faces the monitor. "It's okay. I think I know what's in there. I don't mind if you see."

With that, she clicks open the folder. There's some stuff about where she's from, where she went to college, what people at Rhodes Partners said about her when she worked there.

And an engagement announcement. It's a scanned-in copy of a paper original, a picture of her with some dude, gazing happily into each other's eyes, the text declaring that Anjelica Caprice and Kaleb Younger are going to spend the rest of their lives together.

Anjelica doesn't react to the image. This is *her* pain, but she reacted more strongly to Doc's pain.

And Kaleb... I squint at his image as I realize that it's the neighbor. The one she grew up with, the one who still lives next door to her parents. She was going to marry him. Spend the rest of her life with him.

A bolt of pure, sickening jealousy spears me. I have no right to feel it since this was well before she ever met me and I have no hold on her at all—I explicitly gave that up, in fact —but it's still very real. Very potent.

I hate Kaleb. Mostly for the fact that he hurt her. He could have spent his whole life with her, but he fucking blew it.

She closes the image, clicks through the next few pictures in the folder. A wedding announcement for Kaleb—with someone else as the bride—flashes past, along with several birth announcements for Kaleb's kids.

Kaleb looks like he's having a very nice life. Something that Anjelica would normally cheer, but the fact that Fuchs saved these means that it hurts her. Badly.

This was a life that she wanted at some point. A husband, kids. An intact family. Something I've never known.

No one is saying anything. My hand reaches out, settles on Anjelica's shoulder. I'm surprised to see myself do that, and yet not. She needs comfort. I can at least put my hand on her shoulder.

I hold in my darker emotions. She doesn't need to see those.

"We can close it up." I mean the entire drive, just shut all this down for the night and face the ugly surprises Fuchs has for us later.

I've waited this long to meet my parents. I can wait a little longer if it will spare Anjelica.

She shakes her head. "No, it really is fine. It was so long ago... it's silly that it still hurts."

"It's not silly at all," Doc insists.

Anjelica sinks farther into the chair, breaking our contact. "I should have told all of you about this years ago. Kaleb and I grew up together. Our parents bought houses next door to each other at the same time. Had kids at the same time. We were like a big happy family. Kaleb and I started to have feelings for each other in high school, and it all felt so natural. Of course we'd fall in love."

I'd phrase that differently—of course he fell in love with Anjelica. So why did he leave her? Or what did he do to make her leave him?

Anjelica gives us a bleak smile. "Kaleb and I went to college together, along with a group of our friends. We were going to get married, move home when we were finished... It was like we had this entire happy existence mapped out, one that we were already living."

We all seem to hold our breath, waiting for the bad ending we know is coming. I might be holding my breath the hardest.

"But it turned out that the entire time we were at college, Kaleb was seeing a girl still in our hometown."

Doc gasps. "Oh no."

"Oh, it gets worse," Anjelica says. She's trying for funny, but it's not hitting.

I want her to stop this. We can all fill in the rest; she doesn't have to expose herself like this. I'm hurting so much for her, which means she's hurting even worse.

But she doesn't. It's almost as if getting all this out, walking through the pain, is helping her. "The reason it all came out is because this girl—Harper, his wife now—got pregnant."

That falls like a stone into a bottomless well. Anjelica's not looking at any of us, staring at her knee instead. I want to put myself between her and everyone else, to hide her from this rawness.

But I don't think she needs it. I just… I don't understand how she can do this.

"Oh, Anjelica." Doc covers her mouth with her hand.

"Fuck, man," Finn mutters. "Do you want me to go find this fucker?"

He glances at me as he says it. I can't tell if he's wondering if I already know all this or if he thinks I should be offering to go find this fucker instead of him.

I keep my expression blank. It's none of Finn's business what I know or don't know. Or what I want to do to this asshole who hurt Anjelica.

"Please don't." Anjelica gives a strained laugh. "I already know where he lives—right next door to my parents. When all of it came to light, people… my friends and family, really felt for me. I was the wronged fiancée. But then Kaleb left school, married Harper, moved back home, had a baby. And people stopped being sympathetic."

"You had a right to be angry." I'm furious on her behalf, that this guy wasn't run out of town. That her parents didn't immediately move away from him. Why the fuck didn't they take her side?

"I did, but he and Harper are so happy together. Like, she's more right for him than I was. And they have beautiful children. So our friends slowly forgave him. And when I wouldn't, they couldn't understand. The last year of college was rough for me. I lost contact with a lot of people I thought would stand by me. And I even had to limit contact with my parents, because they…" She tilts her head. "They didn't take his side, but they couldn't keep up the level of anger with him that I had."

"They were the assholes." I want her to be as enraged as I am. "What they did to you was fucked up."

Anjelica shakes her head. "No, what Kaleb did to *me* was fucked up. But he did the right thing by Harper. And I've made my peace with everyone and let go of my hurt. In the end, I wouldn't have been happy living next door to my parents in the town I was born in. I got to come to San Francisco, live out my dreams."

There's quiet as we take that in. Anjelica's more forgiving, more gracious than I can understand, although a wisp of regret lingers in her tone. To simply leave behind what that ass did to her, what her own parents did to her... I could never do it. She's *accepted* her past—I can only discard mine.

"We're so glad you did," Finn says.

"Although we're sorry all that had to happen to you," Doc adds.

This is where I should say something. Give her some token of sympathy. A word. A touch. Anything.

They're all watching me. Finn and Doc expectantly, their expressions urging me to open my mouth and be a fucking human.

Anjelica's watching me with resignation, because she doesn't expect me to do any such thing. She's waiting for me to retreat.

She's cracked open her deepest, darkest secret in front of me and others. And she's already expecting me to fail her.

"Open my folder." I look right at Anjelica as I say it. This is the best I have to offer her. I hope it's enough.

"What?" Finn can't believe it. "You want me to?"

"Open it. Right now." I gesture toward the screen. "Let's see what's inside."

CHAPTER 19

Anjelica told us all about her broken engagement and broken heart so stoically, but now that I've told Finn to crack open my past, she has tears in her eyes.

"Dev." Her voice is thick with emotion. "You don't have to do this."

But I do, because something has convinced me this is what she needs.

"You did it." My resolve never wavers. I look back at Finn. "Do it."

Finn inhales deeply, then clicks on the folder. There are very few files in there, at least compared to what was in Anjelica's folder. Nothing that says birth certificate or parents or anything like that.

Slowly Finn opens the first file. Up pops a scan of the news story from when I was found at the fire station. There are some interviews with the firefighters in it—"no idea who left him"; "we gave him a name"—but nothing beyond what I already know.

Finn and Doc share a glance. They're both smart; I don't need to spell it out for them.

"This is you," Finn says. "As a baby."

All I can do is nod. I've kept this hidden for so long, out of fear of... of pity, I suppose. I don't want pity. I don't want to be so exposed. My breastbone aches so badly I wonder if I've managed to break it somehow.

"You were left at a fire station?" Doc sounds like she can't imagine such a horror.

I stiffen. This is exactly what I wanted to avoid. I don't want to hear how awful it was, how bad they feel about it. I had to live it.

Finn sees my reaction. "It happens," he says mildly. "You... you never told us this."

There's no pity and no censure in his tone. Just a statement of fact.

"I didn't want anyone to know." I can hear how flat my own tone is, although the emotions inside me are anything but. The pain in my chest is so fierce it's hard to breathe.

"Okay" is all Finn says. He closes the image. "Do you want me to keep going?"

No. But Anjelica went on and told them everything. I force my lungs to open. The cool air burns as I breathe in. "Yes."

The next file is a scanned transcript of my entire time at the children's home. Medical records, disciplinary actions, counseling sessions. I couldn't even get these things. But somehow Fuchs did.

This time Doc says nothing. Neither does Finn. They don't need to state the obvious I suppose—that I was raised by the state for my entire childhood. That I never once had a stable home or family of my own.

Somehow not having to explain it makes it easier. I don't have to say anything—these files are doing it all for me. It's almost cheating compared to what Anjelica did.

"That's the end," Finn says quietly when we come to the last page. "Do you...?"

"Yes," I say without hesitation and without inflection. I'm starting to have the terrible suspicion that what I really want

—my parents' names—isn't in here. But there's no way to know until we go through all of it.

This will all be worth it when I find those names. The exposure, the pain, facing their pity—my parents will make it all better.

The rest of the files are exactly what I expect. There are my transcripts from high school and college, even some of my college applications, and lots of interviews; some with the employees at the children's home, some with my teachers and people I've worked with. It's probably the most complete picture of me anyone's ever assembled, but it remains sparse.

Finally Finn opens the last file. It's notes on me, presumably written by Fuchs himself. *Suspect he wrote the algorithm that made them rich* stands out. So Fuchs figured that out on his own.

"That's it," Finn says, his voice even quieter than before.

Doc has been silent the entire time, but her eyes are wide. Anjelica... Anjelica has been watching me steadily, as if she's more interested in my reactions than in whatever Fuchs has put in my file. There's not even a hint of shock on her face.

"Are you sure?" I ask Finn. "Could he have concealed other files somewhere on here?"

My voice is vibrating. I can't help it. I'm holding myself so damn still, waiting so hard for more, I might break. They have to be there.

Finn calls up a command window, types away. After a moment, he shakes his head. "I can do some more testing, but it looks like what we can see is all that's on here."

Every muscle in my body releases at once, like the puppeteer has cut my strings. Somehow I stay upright.

My parents aren't there.

I've lived my entire life without knowing them, but this fresh loss hits me hard, harder than it ever has before. More than just my chest hurts now—every inch of me from the inside out is in pain. I've been chasing this for years, and I thought this time, this time, I've found it. That I can rest after this.

I swear I hear Fuchs laughing at me inside my head. I know he's not, but it feels so real.

"They were supposed to be here," I say, my mouth numb.

"I'm sorry," Finn says. When he does, I learn the true difference between pity and sympathy.

"Thanks." I feel deadened, hollow inside. There's nothing here that I didn't already know. It was all a waste. A complete fucking waste.

Anjelica puts her hand on my forearm. "Let's go home."

I don't know which home she means, hers or mine. Maybe hers since mine doesn't feel like home at all. Frankly, the thought of being alone in my place repels me.

Before we leave, I have to finish this. I look at Doc, who's watching me with mingled sorrow and shock. I don't care anymore though—let her pity me. "Whatever you can find in the archives on your brother is yours. Minerva can help you with access."

She gasps and puts her hand over her mouth. "Thank you," she says through her fingers.

"I should have let you in them in the beginning." I turn to Finn. "Can you comb through them too, find anything with my name on it? I'd appreciate it."

He nods slowly. "Sure thing. I won't open any of it. And I'll… I won't say anything about the rest of this."

I find that I don't care. I don't want it shouted from the rooftops, but if it does get out… I just won't care. "Give everyone else their files from the drive. They deserve to see what's in there."

Finn clears his throat. "About all that…" He shakes his head. "Your childhood doesn't make any difference. It never would have."

That… that makes the heaviness in my chest suddenly lighter. "Thanks."

Anjelica pulls me out then, taking us both to where my car is parked. The night is inky and black, the stars blotted out behind the clouds.

She lifts a hand to my face, then hesitates. I lean into her touch, needing her to anchor me. Once I do, she runs her hands over my face, through my hair. Comforting me in a way I never have been before. The numbness in my mouth begins to fade. The pain inside starts to cool.

"You didn't have to do that." Pride shines out from her voice.

"You were so brave." I never could have done it without her example. "So much braver than I was. Are you… Do you want to talk about it?"

She needs to talk, I know that now. To unburden herself. She's not like me.

"We can." Her finger traces the line of my ear. "We can also talk about you."

"They weren't there." I work my jaw. I guess I need to talk some too. "I was so certain I'd found them, finally, but they weren't there."

"We'll keep looking."

I shake my head. "We're back to square one. All that effort, fucking wasted." My voice breaks on the last word.

"It wasn't." Her hand stills on my cheek. "None of it was wasted. We just have to keep looking for him. And…" She bites her lip. "You told Finn. Finally."

She's giving me too much credit; I didn't tell Finn so much as let him stumble on it. But it's out there now, everything I ever knew about my past.

Anjelica cocks her head, peering intently into my eyes. "Are you okay with that? Do you want to talk about it?"

My instinct is to not talk. To bottle it all back up. Pretend I never told Finn anything.

"It's fine," I say. "It wasn't that awful that he found out."

Her mouth quirks up. "Not so awful, hmm?"

I catch her hand, link my fingers in hers. "I'm never going to be Mr. Extrovert, but yeah, it wasn't so bad. I don't want the whole world to know, but Finn knowing... not so bad."

"And the rest of the Bastards? Would it be so bad if they knew?"

I hold her gaze for a long moment. My instincts are strong, and they are fighting. But my feelings for her are just as strong.

Stronger, actually, because I say, "No, it wouldn't be so bad. And I will tell them."

I don't give her a time line, and she doesn't push. I suppose this first step is enough for her today.

"Good," she says. "Now let's go back to my place and get some rest. We've both had a long day."

CHAPTER 20

I didn't fully appreciate Anjelica's house the last time I was here. I had other things on my mind. Like kissing her. And being rejected by her.

This time it's going to end very differently, so I give myself a moment to take in her space. The space she's constructed for herself.

The curtains are pulled back from the massive windows, and it looks as if the sea could reach inside the living room if it wanted to. The dunes between the beach and the highway are covered with thin, waving grasses and hardy, clinging scrub. The scene is forbidding and beautiful all at once.

Inside the house, Anjelica has made a warm, welcoming counterpoint to the beach outside. A driftwood sculpture sits in the living room, surrounded by couches done in some heavy ivory fabric. There's a mixture of photography and paintings on the walls, some in color, some in black and white, but all with a retro theme. It's all so very Anjelica that it makes me feel... makes me feel like she herself does. Cared for. Welcomed. Wanted.

When I'm here with her, I can hope again. She's right—we can still keep looking for news about my parents. Still keep looking for Fuchs. Not everything is lost.

Anjelica shuts the front door and locks it with a happy sigh. She's got a faint smile on her mouth when she comes into the living room.

"You okay?"

I nod. "It wasn't easy to expose all that, but it wasn't as bad as I expected. Except for maybe Doc's reaction."

Anjelica watches me for a moment. "She reacted that way because she felt for you. Anyone would. It wasn't meant to hurt you."

"I know." I give her a wry smile, one without much humor. "She's allowed her reaction. And I'm allowed mine."

"Fair enough." Anjelica ducks her head. "You think I'm pushing you too much."

Maybe. But maybe it's also what I need. I don't know. "Let's not worry about it now." I hold my hand out to her. I don't want to talk about the past or anyone else. I want it to be just us in this moment.

She comes without hesitation, eagerness in the sweep of her limbs, in the bounce of her step. She bypasses my outstretched hand to land right against my chest.

I curl my arm around to catch her. She fits perfectly against me, her head coming under my chin. She smells like flowers and a hint of cool fog. My entire body relaxes into her. I didn't realize how stressful the past few hours have been for me until just now, when it all releases. Finally, completely releases.

Anjelica breathes into my chest, warming the space over my heart. She sags against me, letting me take all her weight. Revealing her past secrets has been stressful for her too. We both need this.

"You okay?" I ask after a time. I suppose I should have asked before, but maybe this is better, asking after I've held her for a while. Actually helped her get to okay instead of just asking.

She nods, her cheek rubbing against my chest.

"You were very brave."

Anjelica gives a short laugh. "Hardly. I feel more embarrassed than anything. It was so long ago and I was so angry over it and—"

"No." I can't stand to hear her doubt herself and her emotions. "You had every right to be angry. They were all gaslighting you."

I feel her smile into my chest. "How do you know that word?"

"I'm a very enlightened guy. For example, I'm not going to track down Kaleb and make his life a misery, even though he deserves it." His kids don't deserve that, although I'm not sure about the wife—it sounds like she was sleeping with that dickbag when she knew he was with Anjelica. Which maybe isn't as bad as what Kaleb did, but it's still pretty shitty.

But like I said, I'm enlightened. I'll imagine punishing him rather than actually doing it.

"I really have made my peace with it," Anjelica says. "It took a long time, but I did it. Now when my parents mention him, it's more of a twinge than anything else. A remembered pain instead of the real thing."

"They shouldn't be mentioning him to you at all."

"He's a big part of my parents' life. And besides... Kaleb and I wouldn't have been happy together. If I'd married him and moved home, I'd only be half a person. I was able to come up here and find out what I really wanted out of life." Her hand slides up my chest, curls around my shoulder. "I started a career that challenged and inspired me. I joined Bastard Capital. I made partner." Her hand finds my neck, the back of my head, tangling in my hair. "I met you."

I have to kiss her then. Her mouth meets mine eagerly. I want to hear more about what she wants out of life, what she still needs, but that can wait. We have time.

"Where's your bedroom?"

She pulls back and meets my eyes. "We don't have to hold back tonight. I'm... We're ready."

I swallow hard. She's offering me what I asked for the very first time I was here. It was implicit before, but hearing her say it stuns me. Humbles me.

"You're so beautiful." I kiss her temple, the corner of her mouth, the line of her jaw. "So perfect."

She shakes her head. "I'm not."

"But you are. I'll show you." I take her face in my hands. "I promise you'll see how beautiful, how perfect you are to me tonight."

Her gaze shines. She's the very definition of luminous—light and warmth and loveliness. "Oh, Dev." She turns her face, nuzzles my palm.

My cock stiffens, because as sweet as her kiss is, I can imagine her mouth touching other places. Kissing, licking, sucking all of me.

"The bedroom." My tone is urgent.

Anjelica lifts her head, her eyes dark, heated. "This way."

Her bedroom is done in gentle shades, the colors warm and soothing. The pictures on the wall are bright, large paintings of abstract flowers. It takes a moment to recognize that they're Georgia O'Keeffe prints and all those flowers are beautiful, bold pussies.

I want to laugh out my delight, but then I notice the bed. It's unmade, the sheets and blankets tossed around in a way that makes my mouth go dry.

"Come here." I hold my hand out to Anjelica.

This time she comes slowly, her hips twitching and teasing me. First comes off her shirt, then she shimmies out of her skirt. I can see her years of dance training in her every movement, the way she controls each limb so precisely. She's doing it to drive me out of mind and it's working.

Finally, when she's down to only her bra and panties—her

shoes and stockings were gone two steps ago—she puts her hand in mine.

The connection is electric. I tighten my grip, pull her close. Her breasts bob and her thighs quiver as she does, pure gorgeousness in motion.

I drop her hand and reach for her bra, but she slips away.

"No." There's heat and playfulness in her tone. "You have to get undressed. Now."

A smile twitches at the corner of my mouth. "You're giving orders?"

"You like it."

I reach for the hem of my T-shirt. "I do." I pull it off. "But I'm still going to make you pay for it."

She's not listening to what I'm saying; she's wide-eyed as she stares at my chest. One hand lifts, like she wants to touch but can't quite let herself yet.

So I shuck off my pants and boxers.

This time she doesn't hold back. Her hands run over all of me, her breath coming in heavy pants. Even more than her touch, the way she's looking at me is inflaming. Like she's waited as long and as hard as I have for this moment.

I anchor my hand at the back of her head and tilt her face up, kissing her with an urgency I can't control. All my life I've held back, held my emotions in check, but she's smashed all those walls. And with only the slightest flick of her hand.

Her graceful, glorious hands, which are pressed into my chest, her fingers teasing my nipples. I groan into her mouth, my cock painfully hard.

She slips out of my grip, then drops to her knees. The look she gives me from under her lashes almost pushes me over the edge.

"Wait," I grit out. "Your bra, panties." I help her up, then quickly finish undressing her. Her phoenix bursts out from between her breasts, its fiery heart calling for my touch.

I cup her breasts, my thumbs finding her nipples. She lifts

her chest into my touch, and the phoenix looks as if it's about to fly. I bend my head to taste her, her warm skin, tight nipples. She winds her fingers in my hair, holding me hard to her.

I slip an arm around her waist and take her weight, suckling her nipple deep. I can feel her thighs brushing my hip, her lower half bucking against me.

With my free hand, I reach between her legs. "Goddamn," I hiss. "You're so wet and hot. And your clit..." I trace the swollen bud of it and she moans, tipping her pussy up and toward my touch.

She's so close. I work at her folds, rubbing her clit, catching the wild rhythm of her hips. Her juices coat my fingers, my palm, and even touch my wrist. My God, but she's amazing.

"Wait." She shakes her head, pushes against my shoulders. "You're distracting me."

Although it's the hardest thing I've ever done, I pull my hand from between her thighs. Moisture gleams on my skin and hers. "What's wrong?" I'm clenching my jaw so hard I can barely get that out. My cock is even harder than my jaw.

"I'm going to suck your cock." She's staring at me so intently it's a wonder I don't come right there and then. "And you can't stop me."

Jesus, as if I'd ever even try after she said that. I raise my hands and lean back ever so slightly. "I surrender."

"That's right." She goes to her knees with studied deliberation, and the way she holds my gaze the entire time is mind-blowing.

By the time she wraps her hand around the base of my cock, my thighs are shaking. Her grip is confident, and when she looks up at me, she licks her lips.

Holy. Fuck.

I'm still in shock when her mouth closes around my cock. And then I'm in heaven.

She sucks lightly at first, then harder, her tongue working against the underside of my cock. The head nudges the back of her throat and I have to close my eyes, clench my teeth. I force myself to pull back, just a bit.

Anjelica decides differently though. She grabs my ass and pulls me deeper into her mouth.

I start to thrust, slowly at first, then deeper, faster. She's making these sort of humming moans, like my dick is the best thing she's ever had in her mouth and she can't get enough.

I can't get enough. It's the most amazing sensation, her hot mouth wrapped around my cock, her tongue stroking me, her nails digging into my ass. I try to hold back, to hold on to this moment and the pleasure as long as I can, but it's too much. My climax is boiling through me, pulling my balls tight and shooting through my cock like a lightning storm.

While she's still on her knees, Anjelica wipes her mouth like she's never been so satisfied. But I know she could be even better satisfied.

I grab her and sling her over my shoulder in a fireman's lift. She squeals and I take the time to admire the tattoos on the sweet swells of her ass. There's a naughty pinup girl with her breasts bare who's winking at me on one cheek and a four-leaf clover on the other. Fun, happy images—cheeky, you might say.

I deposit her on the bed, and before she can get any ideas, I grab her ankles and pull her so that her ass is on the edge of the mattress. I spread her knees wide and have to take a minute. She's beautiful all over of course, but the pink folds of her, flushed and swollen and wet, are flooring me. I think this view is always going to stun me each and every time I see it.

Then I lower my head, settling my face between her thighs. I inhale deeply, because there's nothing like the scent of Anjelica's arousal. Musky, sharp, and as gorgeous as the rest of her.

She squirms as I kiss my way up her thigh, taking my time with both the right and the left. The scent of her arousal sharpens until it's all I can breathe in.

When I taste those sweet folds, she makes a noise I can't describe. Like she's been waiting for this her entire life but she also can't take it another moment. So I lick again, lovingly tracing each and every fold, circling her clit until her thighs clamp down hard.

I can hear the rustle of the sheets as she thrashes on the bed. I increase my pace, flicking at her clit, shoving my tongue deep, teasing the most sensitive parts of her.

Her hips lift, grinding her pussy against my mouth. She comes with a rush I can taste, her pleasure spreading over my tongue, my lips, my jaw.

She's not even fully released from her climax when she scrabbles at my shoulders, trying urgently to pull me up her body.

"Now please." She's almost sobbing.

I kiss her, lightly, gently, even though I feel the same urgency. I don't want to hurt her. "I'm here. We need—"

"Condoms." She sweeps a hand toward a side table. "Top drawer. Put them in this morning."

"You're a genius." I keep it together long enough to get the condom on, but when I see her spread out on the bed, breasts high, hair tangled, her pussy gleaming from her release, my control snaps.

I climb up her, trailing my mouth over her hot skin. When I reach her mouth, I claim it. Her legs come around my waist, her hips tilt up to welcome me... and I plunge deep. Come home.

Her pussy clenches around me and my cock pulses in reply. I came not more than five minutes ago, but already another, bigger orgasm is building.

I force myself to slow down. She has to come first, which means I need to get control of the climax building in me. But it's so fucking hard because she feels so good. Better than any dream I ever had of her, and there were a lot.

I reach down to find her clit. As soon as I touch it, she's clenching rhythmically around me, little broken sounds coming from her throat.

She's already coming again, and now so am I.

Once my limbs are back from Orgasm Land, I take care of the condom, then slip back into bed.

Somehow we roll together as I slide in, the sheets twisted around us, sweat cooling on our skin. Anjelica shivers as I pull her into my arms.

"Cold?" I try to tug up the blanket, but it's pinned somehow.

She shakes her head. "No, not at all. It was… I don't know what that was. I've never felt anything like that."

"Me either." I settle her so she's covering more of my chest. The blanket comes loose then, so I tuck both of us in.

"Thank you," she says. "For being there for me today."

Something spiked wriggles free and goes careening through my chest. "I didn't do anything." My protest is mostly out of habit.

"You did, and I appreciate it. I know that wasn't easy for you."

"It wasn't easy for you either."

"No, it wasn't." Sleep is thickening her tone. "But see how much better it was when we did it together?"

I can't argue with that, not even if I wanted to.

CHAPTER 21

As happy as I was to be invited into Dev's apartment, I'm glad we're spending the night at my place.

I step out of my own shower, grab my special microfiber hair towel, dry off and use my own face cream, and study myself in the mirror. I've got all my tools here, and I can do my face and hair the way I like. Achieving my look doesn't happen in a man's bathroom.

I pull on my bathrobe and get to work. I start by blow-drying my hair. Setting my hair requires a dry, blank canvas. Ideally, I'd wait a day between washing to set, but I can work with this.

Once that's done, I head into the bedroom and sit down at my vanity. I've always dreamed about having a space like this, with the perfect lighting, outside the bathroom, with a place for all my hair products and makeup. Out of everything in my house, this space feels the most luxurious to me.

Dev sits up in the bed. He's bare chested, and the sight of those lean muscles and dark, wiry hair makes my mouth go dry. I got to sleep with that last night.

I want to sleep with that every night.

I've always wanted to sleep with him, but now that I have, the wanting is a craving. Deeper than a need.

Maybe it's time to reassess my reaction to him. Dev really is making strides toward becoming what I know he can be. He's made the first moves with Finn—only four more Bastards to go. Maybe once he's done there, we can work on expanding his circle even further.

And I can keep helping him. He needs me, he really does. And I need him.

I shiver, a bone-deep shudder, and I remember that I'm only in a bathrobe. First I'll fix my makeup and hair. Then I can continue fixing Dev.

I take my hair out of the towel and start to section it. I won't do anything too elaborate today, just a simple set.

"What are you doing?" he asks.

"I'm setting my hair." I grab the setting lotion and spray the section of hair I've got isolated. With quick motions, I roll the hair up and pin the roller in place. "I curl it, then brush out the curls into the style I want."

"Can I watch? I had no idea how your hair worked."

I smile to myself in the vanity mirror. "Most people don't. Setting curls is kind of a lost art."

He watches intently as I work through the rest of my hair. I know he's never going to need to set his hair, so I find his interest sweetly touching. He's watching because it's important to me.

When I'm done, I look at him in the mirror. "That's it."

He's impressed. "Wow. And now what?"

"I sit under the bonnet dryer for a while, and then I brush it out. That's in the other room though."

"I see." He stretches, and his skin ripples over his muscles. "I should get a shower while you're doing that."

I can only nod, because this all feels so domestic. Like we've always been a couple and this is what we do. We've fallen into this so easily it almost scares me.

Almost, because it mostly feels amazing.

I've set up the bonnet dryer in the dining room so that I

have space to work while my hair dries. I tuck everything under the white cap, turn the dryer on, and open my laptop.

But I can't focus on work. I keep thinking about the USB key and Fuchs's office and where the hell he might be hiding.

I keep thinking we need to go back to the beginning. That what we want to find isn't here at all.

I grab my bag from the chair next to me and rummage through it until I find the list of addresses I made of all the Corvus properties. Running through it again, I linger on all the ones we marked as being especially interesting. Some here in the Bay Area—and there's Hanult's house there—some overseas. And that one in Poland, that's the property with the pear tree.

Out of pure curiosity, I call up Google Maps on my phone and pull up the address. The street view shows what was there when we went—the end of the street and the pear tree with the fence around it. The pear tree is in bloom in the picture.

This time I look behind the tree. There's a high hedge blocking everything from sight. Like whatever is behind the tree is being purposefully shielded from the street.

I zoom out on the map, going to the satellite view. Behind the hedge is a house. There's nothing special about it, but it seems the hedge goes all the way around, blocking it from every line of sight.

An itch begins to build in my brain. I recognize this need for privacy, this obsession with not being seen.

I zoom in on the satellite view, looking for details of the house. There's a car in the driveway, black and sleek. I can't quite tell from here, but it looks expensive. I scroll through the grounds of the house. There're poles every few yards with something atop all of them.

I squint at them. Are those security cameras? I can't really tell. The itch in my brain builds.

"Dev." I don't call very loudly, but I hear him moving in the bedroom immediately.

"What is it?" He comes over quickly, the concern in his voice sharp. He smells like my shampoo. "Are you okay?"

"I'm fine." I point to the phone screen. "This is the property Fuchs owns in Poland. There's the pear tree, but the address is actually all this."

Dev takes the phone from me. "He owns this?"

"According to the records, yes. Who do you think lives there?"

"Maybe no one. Maybe he keeps it empty."

"But there's a car. An expensive one."

Dev looks up and our gazes lock. "We were right there."

I swallow hard. "Right. And he might have been too."

"Son of a bitch," Dev says softly. "Son of a fucking bitch."

"If he was there the whole time..." I sit back in the chair. "After all this..."

Dev sets the phone down. "If he was, you're a genius. You knew where he was all along."

"But I didn't. This is just a guess."

"So far your guesses have been pretty damn good." He looks around. "Where's my phone? We need to get the jet ready. And you'll need to pack."

"We're going right now?"

"Why wait?"

I suppose he's right—he's got a jet, so why not use it?

Just a few hours later, we're in the air. Dev's made some calls, and a car will be waiting for us at the airport. And we've just had the most amazing snack on the plane, a charcuterie board and champagne that was the exact right amount of food.

"Should I prepare the bedroom?" the flight attendant asks.

As many times as I've been on the jet, I've never used the bedroom before. I catch Dev's eye, suddenly feeling very, very wicked. I've also never joined the mile-high club.

He nods to the attendant. "We could use some sleep."

The way he looks at me though says that sleep is the last thing on his mind.

The bedroom is amazing, with a king-sized bed fitted with sage-green sheets. It looks like you could have the best sleep of your life in this bed.

"We won't need anything until we're over Europe," Dev says to the attendant. Meaning don't bother us for several hours.

"Of course." The attendant shuts the door behind him when he leaves.

I'm in Dev's arms the moment after. We kiss with urgency but also exhilaration.

"Have you ever done this before?" I ask.

"Sex on the jet? No."

"You've never even been tempted?"

He goes still. "Anjelica… since I met you, there's been no one. And I mean no one."

I take that in. "You mean not even like for a night?"

He tilts his head as if he doesn't understand. "When I met you, that was it. Forever."

"This entire time you…" I can hardly believe it. Dev is so handsome, so sexy—surely somewhere, sometime, a woman had taken advantage of that. Lord knows I wanted to.

"Yes." He brings my palm to his mouth, kisses the center. "The entire time."

I don't know what to say. It's like finding out you've been the heroine in a fairy tale without even knowing it. The prince has loved you and only you the entire time.

"Dev." I can only whisper his name because this is so enormous. "I had no idea."

Or maybe… maybe I did. Maybe I hoped. I never tried to set him up with anyone, and each time he came to some event alone, a small corner of my heart rejoiced. When he never mentioned a girlfriend or even any dates, I let that small corner hold on to its hope.

"It wasn't something I could bring up in a partners' meeting," he says dryly. He tugs up my skirt. "We'll have to be quiet, you know."

His fingers skim the curls between my thighs, and I start to pant. Already my pussy is hot and achy, and he hasn't even done anything.

He shakes his head as if I've disappointed him. "We have to be discreet." His thumb brushes my clit and I moan. "Clothes on, no noise."

My head falls back as he fingers me harder, my pussy clenching. "I don't think I can," I get out.

"Mmm." He slips a finger inside me, crooking it against the most wonderful spot. "I think I know how to keep you quiet."

He kisses me even as his fingers tease me, pushing me to the edge of an orgasm. I've never come before while I was being kissed, probably because I've never been with a man talented enough to do it.

Dev has talent to spare, and he's not sparing it with me. I come in a blind rush, his mouth fused to mine the entire time.

I don't think a single sound escaped.

Before I've even come down, Dev leads me to the bed.

He pulls me across his lap, my thighs over his and my skirt hiked up to my waist. I reach for his fly, unzip it, and pull out his cock. He's already fully erect, the veins standing out in contrast to the velvet hardness of his skin. The head is flushed purple, and there's a small drop of fluid at the slit.

He tried to be cool and calm while he was fingering me, but his cock tells the real story. Dev's as worked up as I am.

I roll the condom on, his gaze heavy on my hands as they work down his length. Then he's pulling me forward, spreading me open, thrusting inside me.

His cock is thick, but in this position it feels impossibly so. I'm stretched so tight I come from the slightest motion.

He thrusts, once, slow, and I moan, high and needy.

"No," he grunts and takes my mouth. His tongue thrusts in the same rhythm as his cock, all of me straining and stretching toward my climax.

When I come, it's fast, hard, but never ending. Just when I think I can catch my breath, another wave of pleasure crashes over me and pulls me back down.

Dev is there with me, his mouth off mine, his breath hot and quick in my ear. We're clinging to each other, the only thing keeping us upright.

I let my forehead fall to his shoulder, my lungs going so fast my ribs can barely keep up.

"Wow," I croak out.

He makes some noise that might be agreement. Or maybe exhaustion. Or maybe both.

"Do you think they heard?" I whisper.

He laughs silently. "No, I think I got it all."

I lift my head. The gold of his eyes is bright. "How long until we land?"

"Hours."

"How long do you think we can keep quiet?"

One corner of his mouth rises at a wicked angle. "Hours."

CHAPTER 22

Anjelica is holding my hand. It feels strange to have someone touch me in comfort, to be able to touch her in return and take that comfort.

And hope. She gives me hope.

There's about half an hour until we land, and Anjelica is napping since I wore her out in the bedroom. Somehow her hair and makeup remain completely perfect. She touched it up after we got out of bed, but it's still remarkable. I wonder how she manages that, keeping herself so pristine even when she's asleep.

I know she can come undone, and somehow having seen her without her hair and makeup in place means more to me after seeing her keep it intact while she sleeps. She chose to let me see her like that. Chose to let me in when she was vulnerable.

The flight attendant comes up then. "We're starting our descent."

I nod in acknowledgment, then take Anjelica's shoulder and shake gently. "We're almost there." I keep my voice quiet so I don't scare her awake. I shake again, a touch stronger this time. "We're about to land."

It occurs to me that I could kiss her awake, like in the

fairy tales. The flight attendant is gone and won't be coming back until after we land; we wouldn't be seen.

So I do it. I lean over and find her soft lips with my own. I keep it light, a quiet *hello.*

She makes a sleepy noise that sounds like a smile. Without opening her eyes, she asks, "Are we there yet?"

"Almost."

"Then kiss me again."

I do, again and again. Each kiss gets deeper, longer, until we're fully locked in each other's arms by the time the plane lands. I'm pretty sure it's against regulations for us to be doing this while landing, but who's going to stop us?

As the plane taxis to the terminal, we pull apart but keep ahold of each other's hands.

Is this what a true connection is? Touching and being touched, anytime you need it? For all the time you need it?

It's magical. Just like she is.

Anjelica puts her free hand to her mouth. "I need to fix my lipstick. And you…" She raises a laughing eyebrow.

Her lips are bare, which means most of her lipstick must be on me. "Do I look ridiculous?" I look around for a tissue.

"Ridiculously handsome." Anjelica finds a tissue before I do and, taking my chin in my hand, wipes the evidence of our make-out session from my face. I'm tempted to kiss her all over again when she's done—no cleanup necessary now—but the flight attendant comes back.

We're here.

There's a car waiting, a massive German luxury sedan. I want to give a very different impression this time if Fuchs is here. I help Anjelica in and take a moment to admire her, set against the interior of the car. She's in something gray with a severe cut, her mouth a bold pop of red sin in the monochrome of her outfit. It makes me think of bending her over the hood of the car and fucking her until she screams.

Too bad we have other things to do.

The drive seems faster than the last time, but the clock tells me I'm wrong. When the pear tree comes into sight, Anjelica's jaw twitches.

"I want to take this away from him. Give it back to the people." Her tone is low, fierce.

I pull the car to the curb and park. "If it's on the property, technically Corvus owns it. So we could do that."

"Why would he put everything through the company?"

"Because he wasn't expecting someone as smart and dedicated as you are to assemble all the various shell companies and holding firms and get a full list of all the properties."

She ducks her head at the compliment. "He also wasn't expecting someone as clever and devious as you are to take control of the company from right under his nose."

I can only watch her for a long moment. We've both come so far in this, discovered things we've never imagined in each other. "Let's go finish this."

There's a small gate embedded in the hedge. You'd miss it if you weren't specifically looking for it. When I try it, the gate is locked.

But it's a simple padlock, and when I bring the tools out from the trunk of the car—I figured it couldn't hurt to have them—the entire latch comes off easily when I remove the bolts.

"Wow." Anjelica's impressed. "I never would have thought of that."

I savor a moment of pride, then open the gate. "Let me go first."

As soon as I step inside, I see the cameras. Mounted high on poles, they cover the entire yard. I stare straight at one, daring Fuchs to come out.

Anjelica comes up behind me. "Can he see us?"

"Probably." If he's inside. But something in my gut tells me that he is. That he's been waiting for us this entire time.

I hold my hand out for her. She takes it, and as we walk

across the lawn, I keep myself in front of her. I doubt Fuchs has snipers aiming for us, but there was the incident with Minerva and the Caltrain that was never fully explained. He's more likely to try to hurt me instead of her anyway—he probably thinks Anjelica is beneath his notice, a mere secretary. Fuchs has a lot of contempt for those he thinks are beneath him. And he thinks most of the world is beneath him.

We arrive at the front door without incident. Still, my muscles are tense, my heart jittery. Because what if he isn't here? Or if he is, how do I make him tell me what I want to know?

I've come so far, and suddenly failure seems so horribly real.

There's a camera above the doorway. I look up at it as I knock. I do it hard and loud, demanding to be let in.

There's no response. The camera's single eye keeps watching us.

I knock again, just as loud, just as hard. My knuckles are stinging, but I only dimly feel it. Anjelica's hand in mine is more real than the pain.

Still, all is quiet. Even the birds seem to be silenced by my knocking.

"He might not be here," Anjelica says tentatively.

"He is." My answer is grim. I knock again, smashing my fist against the door. "He hears us. He fucking hears us, don't you Fuchs?" That last is a shout aimed at the camera.

Anjelica clasps my arm. "I think you're bleeding. We can try again later—"

The door swings open.

Fuchs has never looked like the absolute asshole he is. This time is no different. He's wearing wire-frame glasses, khakis, and a plain, long-sleeved T-shirt. He's so middle-aged and boring-looking it's fucking offensive. And here he was all this time, right under our noses. Mocking us.

My rage is hot and fast and I'm rushing through the door, grabbing him and pulling him off his feet before I can even think.

"Where are they?" I shake him, making his head bobble like a toy. I can hear his teeth clacking. "Where are they? Tell me now before I—"

"Dev!" Anjelica's voice cuts through my anger. "He can't answer anything like that. Look at him."

I finally do and notice Fuchs is bright red, maybe even a touch purple. I ease my grip and he sucks in a desperate breath. Immediately my fists tighten again. He got an inhale, now he has to talk.

"No," Anjelica says. "You don't have to let him go, but you do have to let him breathe."

I grumble, but I relax my grip. "I'm not going to let go," I warn Fuchs. "Who else is here with you? Guards? Mercenaries?"

He doesn't answer quick enough, so I bounce his head off the wall. "It wasn't hard," I say at Anjelica's look.

"No one," Fuchs gets out. "Just some maids."

I don't know if I should believe him. One more head thump couldn't hurt—

"Don't." Anjelica's read my mind. "Try to ask him now."

I take a deep breath. "A few years ago, you tried to hire me away from the Bastards. Do you remember?"

His eyes are cold, clear. If he's afraid, he's hiding it well. Except for the flush on his skin, you'd never know I was just choking him.

"Of course I remember," he says, his tone as cold as his gaze.

"You had information about my past. Things no one else knew." I was so shocked, horrified really, when Fuchs told me everything he found. I was always so careful to never tell anyone—even the press had never figured it out—but Fuchs had known everything.

I'm not afraid of people finding out now. Not when I'm so close to uncovering the ultimate mystery.

"Records searches aren't difficult." Fuchs's mouth twitches. "For me."

I don't rise to that bait. "You also had other information. Information you wouldn't give me."

His smile comes on slow, like ice forming in the dead of winter, creeping across things and freezing them solid. "Your parents."

Everything about him repulses me, but I hold on. "Yes. I want their names. You promised me that if I'd work for you. I said no and now I'm in control. I hold your company, I even own this house. You'll tell me now."

"I'm not so stupid as to give away my only bargaining chip."

Anjelica makes a small noise behind me. But I knew it wouldn't be this easy.

"What's your opening offer?" I ask.

He shakes his head. "No, it's your opening offer. I can only give you the names of your parents. But you... you could give me back everything you've taken from me."

The offer is surprisingly tempting. I never wanted Corvus, at least not beyond what was in the archives. The company means nothing to me. It's just a burden I have to take apart and sell off. Like scrap.

"That won't happen. But I'm willing to make some kind of deal." The Bastards would kill me if I simply handed the company back to Fuchs. But I can give him something. Something small. "Maybe..." I shrug. "Maybe this house. You can keep living here."

Fuchs laughs in my face. "A house? For your parents? No, I know exactly how valuable that information is to you. You gave yourself away when you took over the company."

My face goes cold. He's right—with all the effort I expended to acquire Corvus, he knows exactly how badly I

184

want those names. How it's eaten at me all these years. How I haven't been able to find a single damn thing on my own.

I'm so goddamn vulnerable it hurts. A fiery ball of pure pain erupts in my gut.

But I keep bargaining. "Fine, this house and Hanult's. I know you want that." I don't tell him we found Pippa there— I'm going to do everything in my power to make sure she escapes him.

"Two houses versus a lifetime of never knowing your parents?" He's mocking me now, and I can't hide my reaction to that—fearful, angry. My entire face has begun to tremble. "No. All of Corvus or nothing."

"Dev." Anjelica's voice is imploring. I can't see her, but I hear the pleading. "You don't have to do this. You have the archives. We can keep searching them."

"Good luck," Fuchs says. "It's buried deep. So deep you may never find it."

"We found the USB key in your office," Anjelica snaps back. "So don't underestimate us."

"And what you wanted wasn't on there." Fuchs focuses on me, dismissing Anjelica. "You'll never find it without me. You know that, which is why you came to find me."

He's right. But he already has too much power here. I need leverage. "She's right. We could just leave you here." I give him another shake to emphasize the point, to remind him who's holding who.

Fuchs doesn't even blink. "No, you can't. I can walk away —I've got nothing left to lose. But you'd do anything to not lose your parents again."

There's a long moment of silence while his words sink in. I can't deny his claims. I need those names. As much as I need Anjelica. Maybe even more, because I haven't been deprived of her my entire life.

"The entire company," Fuchs says. "Take it or leave it.

Wonder forever. I don't care. In fact, I like that idea. Maybe I won't tell you after all. Even if you do offer me the company."

The blind panic that hits me at that is all encompassing. It really is blind—my vision grays out.

"No." That comes out without thought. Even Anjelica's gasp, her reaching for me, can't stop it. "The company is yours. Just give me the names."

I let go of him, step back. He sags against the wall, his shirt wrinkled. He should look pathetic, defeated. He once ruled the tech world, but now he's hiding in a small, unremarkable suburb.

But the light in his eyes is anything but pathetic. Because he knows he can rule the tech world again. I sold him an entire company, and all for two names. Names of people who are probably already dead.

I don't regret it though. Those names are me. Finally I'll receive them and be whole.

Anjelica has her hand over her mouth, her eyes wide with shock. Once we have the names, I'll explain. When we find my parents, together, she'll see that this was right. That this is my happy ending. It's what I've always wanted.

Fuchs slowly straightens up, deliberately pulling his shirt back into place, settling his pants around his waist. It shouldn't be as menacing as it is.

"The names," I say. "I want them now. You have what you want."

He laughs. Out of all the ugly things he's ever done, that laugh is the ugliest thing yet. It makes my stomach turn, reminds me of every lonely moment I've ever had. And there have been a lot.

"The names." Fuchs shakes his head, like he can't believe how stupid I am. "The names."

I wait. We made a deal—I won't beg. Besides, I still hold the company. Nothing's binding. My heart won't slow down though.

Fuchs adjusts his glasses. "There are no names. Never were."

"What?" I know what he said, my brain processed it, but I won't believe it. "You said you had them."

"I lied."

He's so goddamn matter-of-fact I know he's telling the truth. That all this time I'd believed in a lie, probably made up spur of the moment to win me to his cause. He wanted my skills and that was it.

"There was never any information about your parents anywhere," he says. My hands curl and uncurl, one moment a fist, one moment open. "I only offered that to see how low you'd kneel—pretty low, it turns out. I did look for them, because it would have been useful leverage, but there was nothing. Unless they come forward, they'll never be found. And clearly they don't want to be. They don't want you. Never did."

Somewhere beyond the white noise of rage building in me, my mind is calculating angles, distances. The distance of the fireplace poker to my hand. The angle I'd need to swing it at to connect with his skull. How far he might fall before I can raise it again, swing again.

Those thoughts are wrong. I'm not a murderer. But I want to. I want to avenge my parents, as insane as it sounds.

Something breaks through though. Through the heat of my rage and the coolness of my calculations. A tug, the smallest sensation. At the small of my back and at my shoulder. Graceful, beautiful hands I know all too well. Hands that are pulling me back to reality.

"Dev, it's not worth it."

Oh, but it is. What else is left? Finding my parents was everything. And now there's nothing.

Another tug. I take a deep, shuddering breath. Then another.

Fuchs comes into focus first. He's afraid now, fear stark in his eyes. His nose is bleeding too. I don't remember doing that.

"He took them." Is that me? I've never sounded that gravelly.

"He didn't," Anjelica says with infinite sadness. "They were never there."

That pierces the last of my fog. She's right—I've been searching for something that never existed. My parents... they were never there.

I turn and walk out, as empty as when I walked in.

CHAPTER 23

Dev has disappeared.

It's been three days since we found Fuchs—and didn't find Dev's parents—and I haven't seen him since he walked out of Fuchs's house.

When the door shut behind Dev, I looked at Fuchs, who was still bleeding but mostly fine, then went after Dev. But he was gone. The car was there but no sign of Dev. And then suddenly a man appeared and claimed that Dev had sent him to take me home.

Of course I didn't go with him, but he did wait patiently while I called Mark and told him I was in Poland and Dev had disappeared. From there, Mark took over. Turns out the guy really was hired by Dev—he'd put a security team on the house without telling me. Mark kept them there to watch Fuchs and make sure he didn't leave.

I came home. The jet was still at the airport; Dev hadn't taken that either. And when I got back to Bastard Capital, I told them almost everything. Not about Dev's parents—that was his story to tell. But about the search for Fuchs and how we found him.

No one knew what to do. Who was going to arrest Fuchs and for what? We went around and around on that—well, they mostly did, I was too exhausted and numb to talk much —until Elliot decided that Fuchs could just stay there, watched by the security team. If he tried to leave, then we'd do something.

Logan started a search for Dev with Paul's help. The only thing I could do to help was tell them that Dev had had a deep emotional shock and that I was terrified for him.

It was more than terror really. I don't know that there's a name for a fear that runs so deep you go numb. Maybe there is no name.

They were all worried too, of course. They still love Dev in spite of everything. And as we all sat together, united in our worry, I realized that I loved Dev *because* of everything.

I didn't know if he would ever be the man I thought he could be—losing his parents like this, for a second time, would only drive him further into his shell—but I couldn't deny that I loved him anyway.

Mark promised that they'd find him soon and that I shouldn't worry. They sent me home with my assistant, who kept a close eye on me. They must have worked something out, because they keep visiting me in shifts, making sure I'm okay. I always tell them I am.

But it's been three days. And the numb fear isn't going away.

I'm in the atrium, watching as a repairman goes through the sprinkler lines. Turns out Dev hired him before we went to Poland. He's supposed to be the best in the state for designing and building atriums. Dev arranged for him to fly in from San Diego.

"This is a beautiful setup," he says as he fiddles with a sprinkler. "I can't believe some of the orchids you've got."

"Thank you." My manners are automatic. "I'm very proud of it." I put more effort into that.

"You should be." He stands up and dusts off his hands. "That should do it. There was some air in the lines, usually not a problem with outdoor systems, but with places like these, you don't want that. Destroys the serenity."

Yes, I understand that completely. I'm desperate for serenity. "I appreciate it. This place means a lot to me."

He glances sharply at me. "Everything all right?"

No. "Yes. Just a lingering cold."

When he's gone, I stay in the atrium for several minutes. It's warm, beautiful, thick with life. The orchids are cheery, their blooms winking a hello at me.

I force myself to think of only good things. Dev has disappeared before. Lost in work, oblivious to the outside world. And he always comes back. Of course he'll need time to process what happened. And with his history, he'll do it alone.

When he comes back, I'll help him understand that he doesn't have to do it by himself. And he will come back.

I just don't know when.

I haven't said anything to the other Bastards, but I've started my own search for Dev's parents. I started by searching for every ob-gyn in the Sacramento area practicing when he was born, and I'm working my way through them. Most are retired, some are deceased, and no one remembers a young woman alone, scared to be pregnant. I'm assuming a lot about Dev's mom, but it's all I have to go on.

If I can find his parents, maybe that will bring him back.

Georgia pokes her head in. "Um, I'm sorry to bother you, but Helen is here for your three-o'clock meeting."

Right. I'm not looking forward to this. But I head to my office anyway.

Helen looks bad. Hollow-eyed, shrunken shouldered. She barely glances up when I come in.

"You have bad news for me." I decide it's probably best to simply launch right in.

She nods. "The subscriber base just… collapsed. And then

Facebook changed their ad algorithms and we could never make up the loss."

"How much runway do you have?" Runway is shorthand for funds on hand—basically, how long until Helen completely runs out of money.

"Less than a month. Three weeks."

That's not good. Definitely not enough time to fix their ad problems and rebuild their subscriber base.

"How many people have you let go so far?" I ask. We've discussed cuts before, and Helen agreed they might be necessary. She's well past the necessary part.

"None. When it came down to it, I just couldn't."

She's so miserable as she says it, I can't be angry. I understand why she couldn't do it. Even now, some small part of my brain is insisting there's a way out. That some miracle could happen.

But my role here is to be the realist. To give Helen the tough love. Sometimes a dream isn't ready to come true.

I take a grounding breath, bracing myself for what I need to do. "It's time to start shutting things down. Get together severance packages for everyone. Tell them it's time to start looking elsewhere."

She's put together a great team, and they'll find new jobs pretty easily. But the severance packages will help.

Helen says nothing for a long time. She's mourning.

And so am I. I wanted so badly for this company to thrive. It had everything—passionate founder I love, serving an audience that often gets ignored—companies like this are why I wanted to become a venture capitalist.

"I thought this was my chance," Helen says. "I believed in this so much."

I did too. "I know. And you're still amazingly talented. Sometimes... sometimes the stars just don't align."

I should have that printed and hung up in my office.

Because these past few days have proved how true that is. The stars are out of whack for Helen, me, and Dev.

"I'm sorry," she says. "I know how much you wanted this to work out and I… I never wanted to disappoint you."

"You didn't." I'm disappointed, but not in her. I suppose I'm disappointed in fate, which screwed us all over so badly. "And when you come up with your next idea, tell me first. I want to be in from the beginning."

"Are you sure?"

"I still believe in you."

The hope that brightens her expression almost breaks my heart. I wasn't able to make her dream come true, but I made this a little bit easier.

We arrange to meet again next week to go over closing the company. It won't be easy, but we can make sure we do it right.

Once she's gone, I'm tempted to go back into the atrium and just… sit. Sit and wait for news of Dev. But I still have other companies to manage, other prospectuses to go through. And I have my book club tonight. I didn't read the book and I probably won't say much at all, but I want to feel normal. And I need the company of others.

I'm not like Dev. I don't crawl off by myself when I'm hurt.

I force myself to go through some of my emails, trying to write more than one-word replies. When my phone rings, my first instinct is to ignore it.

When I see that it's my mom, my second instinct is to ignore it. But I can't cut myself off from everyone.

"Hi, Mom."

If she hears the bleakness in my tone, she doesn't comment on it. "Hi, honey. I was cleaning out the linen closet and wondered if you want that green tablecloth."

I have no idea what she's talking about. "Which table-cloth? I don't remember a green one."

"Huh. Maybe I got it after you went to college. Do you want it?"

If that's the case, I've never even seen the tablecloth. And while I appreciate the impulse, I'm not sure that I really need another one. "Maybe. Is it really worth shipping it up to me?"

"I remember now!" She sounds like she didn't even hear my response. "We gave Kaleb one for his wedding and I liked it so much, I got one for myself."

The old familiar cold anger comes rushing back. My mother has been using the same damn tablecloth she gave to my old boyfriend. It's ridiculous to even care, but right now I'm too keyed up to stop myself.

Kaleb has a picture-perfect life, with the house and the wife and the kids. The family that Dev never got, that he might never want. Kaleb's not sitting here wondering if the person he loves is hurt or... or worse.

"I don't want to hear about Kaleb anymore."

There's a brief, stunned pause. "Honey, I thought we'd—"

"*You.*" My tone is sharp, high. "You guys are fine with him. You don't mind living next to him. And I'm not angry, not really, not anymore, but I just... I don't want to hear about him. I just don't."

"Okay," Mom says heavily. "I'll try not to. But I thought you were over this."

Tears are burning in my eyes now, but I'm not crying about Kaleb. "It really hurt me when you chose him over me."

I've said this to her before, and I thought we worked all this out, but she doesn't know what Dev means to me, and I don't know how else to get my pain out. I could tell her everything, but if I can't tell the Bastards all Dev's secrets, how can I tell my mother?

"We didn't choose him," Mom says. "We couldn't make our neighbors move away. You chose to stay away. And we respected that. Same as we respected Kaleb's choice to marry Harper and raise his child. What he did to you was wrong, but it would have been worse to turn his back on his child."

"I know that and I agree. But… but you could have handled it differently. Because it felt like you were choosing him. And it hurt, on top of everything else that was happening… it really hurt."

"Oh honey." Mom's fighting back tears, her tone thick. "There were a lot of innocent people caught up in what Kaleb did—his parents, the baby, most especially you. We were trying to do right by those people, but we could have done more to do right by you."

This is the first time my mother's ever said anything like that. Before when we discussed it, she never expressly took any blame in it. I'd let her skirt around the issue in order to make my peace with her.

It means more than I can say to finally hear it.

"Thank you." Now I'm starting to cry. "I know you didn't mean to, but it helps so much to hear that. You can't even know."

"Good, honey. And I'll try my best not to mention Kaleb anymore. I promise. Just… do you think you might be able to come home this year? For Christmas or Thanksgiving or even just a weekend? You won't see Kaleb much."

My tears stop. It's as if the clouds part inside me and there's sunshine again. Not much, but enough to smile about.

Yeah, it is time to go home. Time to finish fixing things between my parents and me, completely. I don't know where Dev is, I can't find his parents for him, but I can do this for myself.

"That would be great," I say. "I want to see all the new stuff Dad's put in the garden. And the curtains you made yourself—I can't believe you sew now. Maybe in two weekends? Would that work?"

My mother inhales so sharply it's almost a gasp. She was expecting me to refuse. "Of course, that would be perfect.

We've got your room ready. It would be no trouble at all. Wait, you can find flights then? It's such short notice—"

I laugh, but not rudely. "Mom, I'm a partner now. We have a jet I can use."

When I remember what I was last doing on the jet, my breath catches. Oh God, Dev has to come back. Before my heart breaks.

"Honey?" Mom asks. "Are you okay?"

I force myself to take a steadying inhale. "I'm fine. And it's settled then—I'll be home in two weeks."

"Oh, we're so glad. Wait until I tell Dad."

I'm glad too. This helped with the numbness, agreeing to visit my parents.

After she hangs up, I stare at the pile of paperwork on my desk. I have to get through it... but I can't stop thinking about Dev and where he might be.

CHAPTER 24

In the end, I took Anjelica's advice: I went back to the beginning.

She meant Fuchs, but it fit me as well. In order to find something, go back to the beginning. So I did.

I wasn't looking for my parents anymore. I wasn't going to find them. I thought when I found them, everything would fall into place. That my past would be something... more.

But learning two names wasn't going to do anything for me. I lived my entire childhood without those names. I had a history even without them. I realized that once I came to terms with what Fuchs had done.

And now I'm back at the beginning.

I look up at the stuccoed two-story facade of the children's home and inhale deeply. Even though Fairytale Town is several blocks away, I can hear the kids running and yelling through the park. And I imagine I can even get a whiff of the Sacramento Zoo.

I already went to see Mr. Jarvis. That was yesterday. He's retired now, spends all his time woodworking. He was so happy to visit with me I was almost ashamed. He saw me in the news, about how I was so successful, and he was so proud of me.

So I told him how much he meant to me as a teacher. I won't say that we cried, but there was a lot of emotion. It didn't feel good exactly. It was more like climbing a mountain—I was exhausted from all the sentiment but kept pushing forward, and at the end I might have reached the top, but I was still really tired. Deep within though, beyond the tiredness, was a golden glow.

I think it will get easier the more I talk to Mr. Jarvis. I promised him I'd keep in touch this time, and I meant it. Afterward, I wanted to call Anjelica, to go over everything with her—how hard it was to take the first step, how I wasn't feeling what I thought I was supposed to be—but I held back.

Mr. Jarvis is part of my past, but he isn't quite the beginning. I want to prove to her I can take the biggest, hardest step on my own. That I don't need her to lean on.

Someday, hopefully, I'll bring her here. But for now I have to do this on my own.

I walk up to the front door and hit the doorbell. From inside comes a long, sharp buzzing, the kind that screams for attention. The door has a keyed entry, and there's a camera watching the stoop, which is way more security than in my day.

The door is opened by a kind-looking, middle-aged woman in jeans and a cardigan. Her glasses are propped up on her head.

"Can I help you?" She's a touch suspicious, and I can't blame her. There are kids here who need protecting, and I'm a strange man just appearing on the doorstep.

"I, um... I used to live here. This was my home."

I've never used that word about this place before. Not once. But as the memories come flooding back, stealing my breath, I realize that it was. Not your typical home and not a home most people would choose, but it was the closest thing I had. And it wasn't all bad.

"Oh." Understanding opens her expression. "I can't let you

go through the home on your own, but I've got five minutes to spare—I can take you around."

I don't ask to see the dormitories—those belong to other boys now, and I'm not going to gawk at their space like a tourist—but I do go through the dining room, the study hall, the library, and finally the kitchen.

Things are different inside—the home underwent a massive renovation a few years ago—but the tree outside the dining room window is still there. I often stared at it as I ate, thinking about math problems. I was a dork.

All the books in the library are mostly new, but I find a copy of *Alice's Adventures in Wonderland* that looks very familiar. I can't be certain it's the same book, but I decide that it is. That something of what I loved lives on in this library.

The kitchen is entirely new. When I had kitchen duty, I usually did the dishes, but there's no sign of the old battered sink I used. Instead, there's a huge industrial dishwasher. I shake my head. Kids these days have it easy.

"Dev?"

At the sound of my name, I spin around. I never told the woman at the front door who I am.

An older lady is smiling at me like I'm the prodigal son come home. For a moment I don't recognize her.

"Dev," she says again, her voice dragging up half-remembered moments. "I thought that was you. Look at how handsome you got."

She holds out her arms and I go into them. As she embraces me and the familiar scent of tea rose fills my nose, it comes back to me.

"Mellie." I sound so young. "You're still here."

She squeezes me tight and my throat closes. "Yep. Still running the kitchen. Although it's a lot nicer now."

She doesn't let go of me, and I don't mind. Mellie was one of the fixtures of the home, the one person who was there all the years I was. She was affectionate to me in her own way, complimenting me when the dishes got done quickly or were exceptionally sparkling. Her job occupied most of her time—feeding all of us was a more-than-full-time affair, even with help—but when she could, she was kind to me.

"I came back," I say. "I had to see the place."

She nods. "Sometimes you have to. I've seen you in the news. You did so well for yourself." There's actual pride in her voice.

"I suppose so." In terms of money, I'm doing great. All the rest of it... that's another story.

"You remember little Davey?"

I do, although I remember him as being the same size as me. I guess we were all little to her. "Yeah. We were usually on dish duty together." We were friends, although I can't remember what we bonded over. Movies, TV shows, girls we liked... I can't bring up a single specific detail, only the way I felt when I was with him. Happy. Content.

He left after a year here. I stayed.

"He came by a few months ago." She holds me at arm's length but doesn't let go of my shoulders. "Or maybe it was longer. But recently. He's doing good. Did you stay in touch with him?"

"No. But I should have." I'm not ashamed to admit that to Mellie since she'll understand. But I wish the answer was different.

"I'll give you his email address," she says. "Do you still make things?"

I don't understand. "Make things?"

"Yeah, you were always building stuff. Out of whatever you could get your hands on. Soda cans, silverware, even plastic straws. I wish I'd kept some of the things you made."

I wish she had too. I wish I had. I vaguely remember that now, shaping bits of scrap to fit my imagination. I remember working in shop class more though. Maybe because I could do bigger and better things there.

"No." One corner of my mouth curves up. "I don't have the time. But I wish I did."

"Well, you're busy. Did you ever get married? Have any kids?"

"No." Anjelica's face appears in my mind. I think… I think I'd be happy with whatever she wanted—marriage, kids, all of it—as long as she wanted to spend her life with me. "Not yet."

Another thing to ask her about once I see her again, tell her everything, ask her for another chance. And confess everything to the rest of the Bastards. I know she needs me to do that. I need to do that for myself too.

"No wife, no kids," I say. "How are your boys?"

A wide smile creases her face. "They have boys of their own now. And a girl. Yep, I'm a grandma. Best job I ever had."

I'm genuinely happy for her. That's what this floating warmth in my chest is. "That's great. Tell them I said hi."

They don't know me from Adam, but this is how you make conversation.

"I will." She sighs, studying my face. "I'm real glad you came today. I'm retiring in a month—if you'd waited much longer, I wouldn't have gotten to see you."

I pull her in for one last embrace. "Then thank God I came today."

She gives me her email and Davey's, I give her mine, and after one last hug, Mellie has to get back to work. And I have to let my reluctant tour guide get back to work too.

As she escorts me to the front door, the woman asks, "Is it much different from when you were here?"

"Some things are very much the same." I realize I don't even know this woman's name and she's just witnessed one of the more intimate moments of my life. But I'm finding I'm okay with that.

Another thing to tell Anjelica.

"Thank you," I say as she opens the front door for me. "This meant a lot to me."

She smiles proudly. "We try our best to be a home for our boys. I know it's hard and we can never take the place of a family, but it means a lot to us when you guys come back and let us know you're doing okay."

I nod. "I am."

I'm okay, but I could be better. And now it's time to go to the person who will make it all perfect.

CHAPTER 25

It's time for the usual Monday-morning partners' meeting, except it doesn't feel so usual.

Yancy can't get the teleconference equipment to work, so Elliot and Paul can't call in. Logan is home because the baby is sick, which leaves just three of us—Mark, Finn, and myself.

Dev still hasn't reappeared. If he wanted to break my heart, it's working. I'm sick with worry. It's been five days. Five whole days. I can't take much more of this.

The other two look just as bad. Mark's got dark circles under his eyes, and Finn can't stop playing with his pen. No one says anything.

Finally I sigh. "Nobody's heard anything? At all?" My voice cracks on the last word.

"If we had, you'd be the first to know," Mark says gently. "He's gone off-grid before."

It's cold comfort and Mark knows it.

"At least Fuchs is still where we left him." Finn's staring at the table, his pen rolling through his fingers.

"I don't care about Fuchs," I say. "Dev's never disappeared like this."

Mark steeples his fingers. "Do you think... I know you

don't want to betray his trust, but if you could tell us what was going on, it might help."

It might. I've been wrestling with whether to tell them everything all week. If we had more clues, like we did with Fuchs, we might find him.

What did I tell Dev? Go back to the beginning. But he'll never go back to his own beginnings. The promise of his parents was a lie, and that was the only thing from his past he cares about. The rest is nothing to him—he'll never go back to it.

So where is he?

Mark's watching me, waiting for an answer. So's Finn.

I'm torn. Torn between my loyalty to Dev and my worry for him. And my loyalty to the Bastards. Any way I choose, someone's going to be upset.

Dev's not here. Maybe it's time to decide for him.

I open my mouth. I'm going to tell them everything. I think.

Before I can, Yancy comes back. "I got the video link working."

Finn frowns. "I thought we were just going to leave it."

"Oh no." Yancy gestures toward the door. "He— That is—"

"I told her to get it working," a deep voice says from the doorway.

I look up. Dev's there and my heart... Oh, my heart. If I thought it hurt before, it's nothing compared to actually seeing him. He came back.

He looks sad, solemn. But alive and intact. I want to kiss him for coming back and yell at him for disappearing.

I want so many things with and from him.

Mark is rising out of his chair. "Where the fuck have you been? We've all been freaking out over you. And Anjie..." He gestures to me, his mouth a grim line.

"You can't keep doing this, man." Finn shakes his head. "It's fucked up. And we're all sick of it."

"So am I."

That brings us all up short.

"You are?" Mark asks.

Dev nods. "It's time to do this. Elliot and Paul should be calling in any moment, and Logan ought to be— Here he is."

Logan comes in behind Dev, looking exhausted. "This better be good. I haven't slept in twenty-four hours."

Dev says nothing, merely looks at me. When our gazes connect, it's like a current snaps between us. No matter what happens, we'll always react like this to each other. We always have.

"I'm sorry I didn't call." His voice is pitched only to me. "I would have, but I wanted to go back to the beginning. On my own, without you having to push me. And when I came back, I realized I had to do this for you before I could do anything else."

"What exactly are you doing?" I ask quietly.

"What you always wanted me to. What I should have from the very beginning."

He takes his seat then, just as Elliot and Paul flash up on the screen.

"Everything okay?" Paul asks. "I thought the video feed wasn't working."

"I fixed it," Dev says.

They both blink in shock when they hear his voice.

"You came back," Elliot says.

"Of course." He steeples his fingers. The entire room is focused on him. Even Yancy. "I have to tell you all something. About why I acquired Corvus. It wasn't… it wasn't to unseat Fuchs or to dismantle the company. I didn't care about that."

Their expressions have gone stony, and I don't blame them. Fuchs has personally hurt all of them, gone after what they most care about—Dev is making it sound like he doesn't care about what happened to them.

"You're speaking in the past tense," Elliot points out.

"We'll get to that. For now, just know that the Corvus archives are open to all of you. Completely. Take whatever you need, whatever might help. We can discuss later how we'll all work together to dismantle the company."

Some of the tension leaves the room. But not all.

"So why?" Finn crosses his arms. "Why buy Corvus? You wanted into the security business?"

Dev shakes his head. "No, I don't care about Corvus's mission either. I never told you this, but back when we were first starting Bastard Capital, Arne came to me with a job offer. He knew I wrote the core of the algorithm, and he wanted my skills. He... offered something I wanted very badly if I'd join him."

Dev's gaze is remote, like he's lost in memory. And a touch sad. His expression is definitely not blank—he's invested in what he's saying. He's here, emotionally present.

"What was it?" Mark asks. "That Fuchs offered you?"

I hold my breath, because until he says it, I can't quite believe he's going to do it. After all this time, after wishing so badly he would... he still might not do it. The words haven't left his mouth yet.

"The identity of my parents."

The way he says it is stark, bare, but it lands like a grenade. My heart starts tripping over itself.

"Your... your parents?" Logan's mouth falls open. "You never knew them?"

He's too far away, but I so wish I could reach for Dev's hand, give him some comfort, some reassurance. This can't be easy for him no matter how tightly he's holding himself together.

"No." There's a hairline crack in that. "I was left at a fire station when I was only a few days old. No sign at all of who

I was or who my parents were. Nothing was ever found. My name came from the firemen who found me."

"Fuck." Mark looks like he's been punched in the gut. "Fuck, man. I'm so sorry."

I stiffen, because that's pity and exactly what Dev never wanted. But he merely shrugs.

"Thanks. I had a few foster families when I was very young, but I spent most of my childhood in the Sacramento Children's Home."

His voice seems to be getting stronger. Certainly he's speaking with less hesitation, like the story is coming easier to him.

Mark rubs his chin. "That's… that's rough, man."

There's a sense of weight in the air, all of us carrying our horror and shock at Dev's story. Sharing the load of it. Taking it from Dev's shoulders.

"It was," Dev says. "But I made it to college, and eventually I met you guys. It was like… like I'd always imagined a family might be like. But I'd learned not to talk about my past—people get weird when they find out you spent time in a group home—and I never thought I could bring it up. It was a family, but I didn't know how to be in a family."

Mark sucks in a sharp breath, and Finn can't stop clearing his throat. They all look like they're fighting back tears.

"We, uh, we feel the same," Logan says. "About the stuff you said."

I roll my eyes. "Oh, grow up, all of you. You love each other. You're grown men—you can say it!"

They all look at me in shock.

"Isn't that what I said?" Logan seems genuinely baffled.

Dev's wearing a small smile. "No, I get it. And I, uh, feel the same about everything I said. I should have told you guys everything from the beginning instead of being a close-mouthed asshole."

"Yeah," Finn says. "You should have been an openmouthed asshole."

I can feel them start to knit back together in that moment. The emotions got out, they all got close to crying... and now the insults are back. If the insults are back, everything will be fine.

I sit back in my chair and release a shaky breath. It's happening, everything I ever wanted for Dev. He finally did it.

"So that's why you were so determined to get into the Corvus archives," Mark says. "You thought you'd find what Fuchs had on your parents."

Dev nods. "I wasn't going to give him what he wanted, but I had to get their names."

"And that's why you were looking for Fuchs," Elliot says. "You thought he'd tell you where to find it in the archives."

"We found him, yes." Dev's gaze focuses on the wall. "But he'd lied. He never had the identity of my parents. He only said it because he knew it was what I most wanted in the world."

There's a long beat of silence.

Finn is the first to break it. "They... they might still be out there. I can find *mostly* everything."

Dev shakes his head. "No, they're not. I've spent the past few days coming to terms with that. And revisiting my past. I'm..." His eyes lock with mine. "I'm fine with it. I never had their names, and I don't need them to be happy."

Meaning... he needs me to be happy? My cheeks are cold and hot all at once. He can't do this now... can he?

He must see all the questions in my eyes because he silently mouths *Later* to me. I catch the word, hold it close to my heart, right over the phoenix there.

We've waited so long for this—later is a promise I can believe in.

CHAPTER 26

Anjelica slipped out an hour ago, leaving the rest of us on our own. I guess she figured we needed some Bastard-only time, although she's as much a part of us as everyone in this room.

Mark has broken out some whiskey, and Elliot and Paul are still on the video chat. It's almost like the old days when the six of us were in that stuffy, shitty garage. Which we're reminiscing about.

"Do you remember that Thanksgiving we had in that place?" Mark asks.

Logan immediately starts laughing. "And we thought we'd cook for ourselves? Yeah, I remember."

I remember it too. It was the first Thanksgiving I spent with something like a family. Which maybe isn't fair—at the children's home we always got a proper Thanksgiving feast, thanks to Mellie—but it was definitely the first that felt like I thought a Thanksgiving did to everyone else.

"How did we manage to cook only half the turkey?" Finn muses.

I laugh because it was the weirdest thing—half the turkey was just fine, and the other half was pink as hell. And it was straight down the turkey's midline, like that side of the oven was ice cold.

"The mashed potatoes were really good though," Paul says. "I can't remember who made those."

I lift my hand. "I did. I learned from the lady who ran the kitchen at the home."

There's the barest hiccup, like they're all recalling *Hey, that's right, we just learned Dev grew up in a group home,* but then it's over.

"And Finn bought a pie for each of us," Mark says.

"Pie's the best part," Finn says. "And nobody could agree on what they wanted. So I got one of each."

That's right—I had an entire peach pie all to myself. It seemed pretty decadent, and I ate every bite that day, just because I could. The turkey might have been ruined, but that pie was delicious.

"We should do that again," Logan says. "Have Thanksgiving all together."

"Can we cook the turkey this time though?" I ask.

Finn snickers. "If you insist. Might ruin the magic though."

"We already know Finn's bringing the pies," Paul says.

We laugh together, bound by our shared memories. Anjelica was right—I never should have let the distance grow between them and me. I should have told them from the very beginning. They wouldn't have cared. They don't care.

But I guess I needed time to learn that. Learn to trust, really trust someone. And I suppose I needed to lose the illusion of my parents before I could.

Suddenly I miss her. Hanging out is great and I've missed it… but I miss her too.

As if the guys can sense that, the mood changes.

"So what are we going to do about Fuchs?" Mark asks.

"I joke a lot about shallow graves and the desert," Finn says, "but I'm not joking now."

"Except we'd be the first suspects if they ever found him." Typical Elliot, pointing out the legal pitfalls.

"I'm willing to take the chance," Logan says.

"I could fight an extradition," Paul says.

That's when I get the idea. "I know what to do." I turn to Elliot. "Have Emily turn him in. It'll help with her case, won't it?"

He blinks as he ponders that. "It should. They want him more than they do her. He won't go to jail, but I know there are some very irritated people at the NSA and the CIA who want to talk to him about his data leaks. And Congress wants to haul him in for some testimony." He nods. "It can only help."

"Then do it," I say. "And whatever Emily needs from the archives, it's hers. She knows better than I do what's in there."

Elliot actually smiles. "Thanks. That means a lot."

I'm happy I can help. I really am. "Sure thing."

"I can ask Emily about what there might be about your parents," Elliot offers. "If it's all right with you."

I shake my head. "Feel free, but there's nothing there." The more I say it, the more serene I feel about the whole thing. As if I'm finally done mourning the parents I never knew. "She's got bigger things to worry about."

Elliot looks behind him. "Speaking of that, I should head out soon."

"Me too," Mark says.

That's right—they all have people to go home to. And so do I now.

Logan picks up his phone, smiling when he sees what's there. "Aurelie's finally sleeping."

"Aren't you supposed to sleep when they do?" Mark asks.

"That's what they say. It's harder than it sounds though."

Mark makes a noise in his throat. "I guess we'll find out soon enough. January's pregnant."

I'm insanely happy for him and jealous all at once. I've never really thought about being a dad. It seemed as unlikely as going to the moon. But thinking about a future with Anjelica has me recalculating distances that once seemed impossible.

I have to get to her. I have to talk to her.

But first I need to congratulate Mark. The rest of them are slapping his back or cheering him on from the video link. I get up, give him a short hug. "Congratulations, man. January and the baby are lucky to have you."

"Thanks." Mark is smiling like crazy. "It's been wild. Thank God we already started planning the wedding."

"First a wedding, then a baby." Logan grins. "Welcome to the club. And when are the rest of you assholes joining?"

Finn immediately starts spluttering, Paul merely smiles enigmatically, and Elliot shakes his head.

"Doc and I are going to do things on our own schedule," Finn says. "I already proposed anyway."

"You sound as bad as my mother," Paul says.

Elliot's tone is dry as hell. "Once we don't have a warrant out for our arrest, we'll think about it."

Mark and Logan share a look.

"Elliot's the only one with an excuse," Mark says.

All of them turn to look at me.

"I should be going," I say.

"Tell Anjie we said hi," Finn says.

They all start snickering. Then full-out laughing.

"It only started after she made partner," I shout over the noise.

"Oh right." Logan rolls his eyes. "You guys were mind fucking from the very beginning."

I'm trying my best to hang on to my dignity, although I suppose I deserve this. "There was no mind fucking."

"Yeah, there was." Finn taps his temple. "Fucking with *your mind.*"

Something about the way he says it just kills me. I laugh

so hard I have to put my face into my hands. It's completely ridiculous and I love it.

Finally I look up and nod. "Yeah, she was fucking with my mind. Hopefully I've got myself sorted out enough for her though."

Mark gestures to the door. "Go on then. Get."

"But if you hurt her..." Logan's voice is quietly menacing. "We'll kill you."

Finn's stare is cold. "Desert. Unmarked grave."

I turn toward the door. "That's more than fair. Wish me luck."

They all stand up. I feel like I'm being sent off to war. They all insist on shaking my hand before I leave, and I realize we're all a little buzzed. Maybe more than a little buzzed. I'll have to call a car.

Logan grins. "Good luck."

"Take care of her." Finn gives me a nod as I head for the door.

"I'm so glad I'm not in the room for this." Elliot rolls his eyes, trying not to laugh.

"Me too," Paul agrees.

"Godspeed," Mark says.

"What the fuck does that even mean?" Finn asks.

As I slip out, they start up again. It's one of the best sounds I've ever heard.

CHAPTER 27

This time when Dev knocks on my front door, I'm ready.

The ocean is quieter tonight but still a dull roar. It can never be entirely silent. It reminds me of my own heartbeat —sometimes quiet, sometimes loud, but always there.

When the knock comes, my heart reacts but the ocean doesn't. I knew he was coming and I'm ready, which is why my pulse is jumping inside me. It's time for just us now.

He's not smiling as I open the door, but he does have one arm braced against the doorframe. It highlights the lean strength of him in a way that makes my mouth dry. He's so much more relaxed this time... but he's also holding back. Waiting for me.

"How did it go?" I ask. "Afterward?"

He purses his mouth as he considers it. "I think we're okay again. It's not... not one hundred percent, but we'll get there." His gaze drops. "You were right all along. About everything."

I put my hands over my mouth for a moment, because it's everything I wanted for him. To be open with those who love him. All of them. "You had to tell them in your own time, in your own way. I gave you a push, that's all."

"You did a hell of a lot more than that."

I cross my arms. He's not getting off that easily. "You can't disappear like that. We were all worried sick. Especially after what happened. You just... you left me." My voice breaks and I let it. He needs to know how badly he hurt me.

He reaches for me and I let him. Even when he's the one who caused the harm, his touch still comforts me.

"I'm sorry. I'll admit I was an asshole for leaving you. When Fuchs revealed he'd only been fucking with me... I lost my mind. I remembered to call the security detail, to make sure you got home safely, and then I found a place to get really, really drunk."

I sniff and wipe my eyes. "You get drunk?"

"Not very often. I made up for lost time."

"And the rest of the week? You were just drunk?"

He smiles wryly. "No, although it did take me a full day to get over the hangover. I went home and I did exactly what you said. I went back to the beginning."

I frown. What beginning does he mean? "But we'd already found Fuchs."

"My beginning."

My breath catches as I realize what he means. "You talked to Mr. Jarvis?"

He nods. "You were right: he remembered me. And he was really glad to hear from me."

I knew he would be. Who wouldn't be proud of what Dev had done with his life? "How did you feel?"

He takes a deep, contemplative inhale. "It was awkward, but at the same time good. Like, he was so proud of me it made me uncomfortable, but it also felt great to hear. Is that how it's supposed to be?"

I smile through my unshed tears, because that's such a Dev thing to ask. "Yeah, that's normal. You'll get used to it."

"It'll be easier next time," he says. "I promised to help him set up his home machine shop." He looks away, then back at me. "I went to the home too."

"Oh, Dev." I reach up to stroke his cheek. "Was it hard? I would have gone with you."

He shakes his head. "No, I had to do it myself. It wasn't as bad as I'd imagined. They've changed things, but not everything. The lady who ran the kitchen was still there—she was happy to see me." He smiles as he remembers, and my heart splits with a silent crack.

He did it. He went back to the beginning.

I search his face, trying to tell him how I feel about what he's done. It's so massive I wasn't certain he could do it. But he did.

"I love you," I say.

The expression that crosses his face is indescribable. It's like watching a wish being granted but only better. He cradles my face, his gaze holding mine.

"Damn," he says softly. "I wanted to be the one to say it first."

Oh, if I wasn't already in love with him, that would do it.

"I've loved you from the first moment I saw you," he says. "Even though I don't believe in that stuff. But I couldn't shake it. You're the bright spot in my soul."

I release a teary hiccup. I'm so happy I'm crying and laughing at the same time. "How am I supposed to top 'bright spot in my soul'?"

"You don't have to. You only have to be you."

He lowers his mouth to mine, and we kiss for long moments. It's like our first kiss—consuming, enchanting, a kiss to remember for a lifetime.

When we pull apart, he sets his forehead against mine. "I'm so sorry. I won't leave you again."

"I know."

"They told me about the company. I'm so sorry."

I try to shrug, but my shoulders are too tight. "It's one of those things. More companies fail than succeed, so I knew it might happen."

"Hey. Don't do that. You were really excited about this. Be sad about it. It was a shitty thing that happened."

Dev is telling me to let my emotions run free. I have to smile, because it's so unexpected. "I am sad. But there's hope too—I told Helen this wasn't her only chance to make her dreams come true and when she comes up with an even bigger and better idea to call me first."

"She will," he says. "You have an eye for talent."

That makes me feel better about the whole thing. I suppose any of the Bastards would have said that, but it means more coming from Dev.

"I tried to look for your parents," I say. "Your mom, actually. She might have visited a doctor at some point, so I started there."

His expression softens. "Oh, Anjelica." He runs a finger down my cheek. "Thank you. But... but I don't think they'll ever be found. And I'm all right with that. If I never find them, I'll still be the same person. A better person though, thanks to you."

I swallow hard, because it's sad but also a relief. I still hope we find them someday, but I'm glad Dev's accepted that we might not. And that he's okay with it.

I set my head against his chest. A yawn catches me unawares. It's only the early afternoon; I shouldn't be sleepy. In fact, I can think of something that might keep me up...

I tilt my face up and catch his eye. "Feel like an early bedtime?"

Instead of slinging me over his shoulder, he frowns. "There's another thing I need to ask you."

I'm not nervous, but he seems to be. "What?"

"I want you to come with me. To see the home. I had to do the first time on my own, because... because I just had to. But I need you to see it too."

I run my hand over his cheek. "Of course. I'd love to see where you grew up. I should ask you too... I'm going home in a few weeks to visit my parents. You can come if you want. You'd probably have to stay in a hotel since they're kind of old-fashioned, but…" I take a breath because I said all that too fast. Dev simply waits. "I want you to meet them. If you want to."

"I'd be honored. I've never met the parents before." His expression darkens. "Will you have to see Kaleb?"

"Probably. But it will be fine. He doesn't want to see me as much as I don't want to see him. We'll say hi, tell him how cute his kid is, and that will be it."

"If you're sure. We can always invite your parents here, take them to Napa for the weekend. I'm sure they'd be impressed by Logan's winery."

It's a lovely offer, but… "I haven't been home in years. I have to go."

"Then I'll go with you. And I'll be very polite to Kaleb."

I laugh because he's glowering right now. "Dangerously polite? Murderously polite?"

One corner of his mouth ticks up. "Okay, I'll probably just be reserved. If that's all right."

"It's more than fine."

He wriggles his eyebrows. "So, about that early bedtime…"

When I laugh, he slings me over his shoulder. He already knows the way to the bedroom.

"So when should we move your stuff in here?" I ask when he sets me down.

"If you're here, then there's nothing else I need."

I swallow hard at the intense heat in his eyes. I was worried about being his only thing, but being his everything is pretty good. Better than good. Better than anything I could ever want.

I raise an eyebrow. "If you think I'm sharing my clothes…"

He's still laughing when we fall back together on the bed.

CHAPTER 28

When we get out of the car, Anjelica immediately reaches for my hand. When her fingers close on mine, my heart fills. This visit isn't a homecoming, but walking up with Anjelica's hand in mine makes it feel like it could be.

Her hair is done in loose curls, the sides caught up with tortoiseshell combs in the shape of dragons. Her dress is light yellow, like morning sunshine, and baby dragons play at the hem of her full skirt, playfully setting fire to things. Her outfit is both cute and dangerous, and it makes me happy even as I imagine taking it off her tonight. Or even earlier.

"They renovated it recently?" She peers up at the facade through her sunglasses.

"Yeah. The grounds are all different and the backyard is completely changed, but the outside was just freshened up."

"My parents changed their garden too," she says. "My dad will probably give you a tour."

We're comparing childhood homes. I've never done it before. Nothing about my childhood was normal, but I'm learning how to talk about it. I'll probably never share with strangers, but Anjelica is an entirely different matter.

I've already called ahead and made sure our visit was okay. We won't stay long—all these people have important, demanding jobs to do—and we won't see the dorms and most of the kids are at school, but I can share at least some of it with Anjelica. And she can meet Mellie.

Anjelica is mostly silent through the tour. Which is good, because I don't think I can talk much this time. The first time I went through here was like a shock, a leap into cold water. I could only take everything in.

This time there are memories. Good ones, but dark ones too. Things I'll probably never tell Anjelica about because they'll only upset her. Things that remind me I had reasons for never coming back here.

I don't even realize I'm breathing hard until Anjelica squeezes my hand and asks very quietly, "Okay?"

"Yeah." I focus on her, how much I love her, how bright my future is with her. "Bad memories."

She squeezes my hand again, and my breathing slows to normal.

The woman taking us around hasn't even seen; she's describing all the new features in the library. I find the copy of *Alice's Adventures in Wonderland* I noticed before and show it to Anjelica. "This was here when I was," I say only for her.

She runs a hand over the cover. "Did you like it?"

"It's all about math, so yes."

Anjelica has to smother her laugh as we move to the next room. I notice that the bad memories are still there, but they're a touch dimmer. I can breathe normally.

We head to the kitchen next. At the doorway, the woman in charge of us says, "I'll let you catch up—just head to the front door when you're done."

When we walk in, Mellie actually claps when she sees us. "You brought her!" She hugs Anjelica, then steps back to assess her. "How did you end up with someone so beautiful?"

"I got lucky," I say. "Very, very lucky."

Anjelica winks at me. "And don't you forget it."

"I never will," I say quietly.

Her mouth purses and she looks like she might tear up, but she holds it together. And then Mellie starts to fuss over her and Anjelica asks her all kinds of questions about running the kitchen. I look around while they talk. There're no bad memories here, and not only because it's been completely redone since I left.

I'm glad I made Mellie happy by bringing Anjelica here. And I'm glad I brought Anjelica, just so she could see. I don't want to be the only person in my life who knows about this place anymore.

"So…" Anjelica gives me a mischievous look. "What was Dev like as a kid?"

No one has ever asked that about me. Not once. It feels good? Intense? Both at once? I'm not good at naming these things.

Mellie smiles. "He was a very good boy. Always did his chores without complaining. And smart! He fixed the dishwasher once."

I forgot about that. "It was easy. One of the hoses had come loose."

"He's still very handy," Anjelica says.

All right, that's enough of this. I can only take so many compliments. "I emailed Davey," I tell Mellie. "He said to say hi."

"Did he send you pictures of his baby? What a doll that child is."

I nod. "He did, and the baby is very cute."

Mellie fixes me with what I guess is supposed to be a stern look. "Your turn next."

Anjelica ducks her head, but not before I see the flush of pink on her cheeks. That's going to be an interesting conversation. But whatever we decide, as long as Anjelica's happy, I'm happy. All I want to do in life is please her.

"We'll see," I say. "But if we do, you'll be the first to get pictures."

Anjelica nods. "And you can tell me more about when Dev was little."

Reluctantly I check my watch. "We should be going. We're not supposed to be here that long."

Mellie and Anjelica hug and exchange information, and I hug Mellie too. Our goodbyes are bright, light with the expectation that we'll all see each other again.

When we get outside, we walk slowly to the car. Anjelica is holding my hand again. We've got nowhere to be for the rest of the day, which is rare for us.

"So that's that," Anjelica says. "Do you want to talk about it?"

I shake my head. "It was enough that you went and met Mellie. That meant a lot to me."

"It meant a lot to me too." She swings our joined hands. "So what now? You've told everyone about your past, you found Fuchs... What will you do with Fuchs?"

"Emily is going to tell the government where Fuchs is."

"What's going to happen to him next?"

"Honestly? I don't care. I spent all those years obsessed with him and now..." I shrug. "I took his company from him, and now I'm dismantling it. We've exposed a lot of the awful shit he did, and if he has to testify before Congress, he's finished in tech. So... he's done."

"Good," Anjelica says with relish. "I guess there's not much left then besides clearing Emily's name and finishing the shutdown of Corvus."

I frown because it's just occurred to me that there's actually a lot left to be done. The most important thing really.

I pull Anjelica to a stop and turn so we're facing each other. "I've been waiting to ask this for a long time. Almost as long I've waited to tell you I love you. I admit, I never thought much about marriage and a family, not with my background. But when I do, Anjelica, you're the only person

I could ever imagine doing that with." I can't stop myself—this next has to come out. "Anjelica, will you marry me?"

I don't have a ring, I'm not on one knee, but suddenly I can't think of a better place to ask her than here and now.

She opens her mouth but says nothing.

Oh shit. I went too fast. This wasn't the place to do it, we haven't even moved in together, and I've only just shown her the place where I grew up.

I've completely misread the situation. Again.

But then a light comes into her eyes, more of a glow, and she says, "Yes."

That's it, just yes. But it's more than enough.

I kiss her then, in front of the children's home, the street, the entire world. And I don't feel a bit exposed.

When we break off after I don't know how many minutes, she smiles up at me, all soft and fond. Like I'm her Prince Charming or something. "I'm not taking it back," she says. "Even if you end up hating how much time I take to do my hair."

"It'll never happen."

"Or hate my cooking."

"Again, it won't happen."

"I *will* take up more than my fair share of the closet."

"Good." We start walking to the car again, our hands swinging between us.

"And the shower shelves. You'll be lucky to have space for a bar of soap."

I lift our hands and press a kiss to her knuckles. "There's nothing you could say that would keep me from loving you. For always."

She smiles like she's just won the lottery. Or something even better than that.

But I'm the one who's really won. Everything I could ever want.

EPILOGUE

I never expected that my wedding would be the biggest event ever in Silicon Valley history—I was thinking something smallish in our family church back home, with most of the guests being my high school friends.

But I was imagining those things back when I thought I'd marry Kaleb. Once that was over, I stopped dreaming of weddings.

When Dev proposed, I dreamed again. I started small— the Officers' Club in the Presidio, an off-the-rack dress, the guests our closest friends.

But somehow the wedding planning turned into a snowball. And then a snow boulder. And finally an avalanche.

I'm not upset. I'm more amazed that so many people want to celebrate our marriage. And see and be seen with us, to be honest. I won't lie—it's kind of flattering.

So here we are, on day three of the celebrations, finally getting to the actual ceremony. There was a party in Mountain View the first night, with all the tech-world royalty in attendance. Except, of course, Arne Fuchs, who's serving a very long sentence in a very secure federal penitentiary. Fuchs is locked up, Emily and Elliot came home, and the rest of us… we're all great.

Last night we had a massive ball at the opera house for family, friends, and business partners to celebrate our upcoming wedding. Tonight it's much smaller. More intimate. Just about a hundred people, our most beloved friends and family, gathered at Stern Grove to watch us exchange vows.

I haven't seen Dev all day, and I'm eager to finally walk out of this dressing room and begin the rest of our lives together. I'm also eager for him to finally see my dress.

In the end, I didn't go off the rack. I found a seamstress who does the most amazing retro dresses, all designed by her, and commissioned a custom dress. The ivory silk is heavy, but it clings to my curves in a glamorous, slinky way. I look like a star from the Golden Age of Hollywood, only a touch more modern, a touch sexier. I'll have to find a place to wear the dress again; it's too beautiful to only wear once.

The wedding planner—one of them, we had to hire two— pokes her head into the dressing room. "Are you ready?"

I've never been more ready. But all I say is yes.

My mother helps me gather up the veil, which trails several feet behind me. I wanted an extravagant, ridiculous veil to go with this dress, and I got it. The front hangs all the way to my knees. I'm probably going to have to help Dev flip it back.

Or maybe not. He's a very handy guy.

"You're so beautiful," Mom says as we leave the dressing room. Her eyes are bright with tears and she can't stop smiling.

"Thank you." I squeeze her hand. "It's because I'm so happy."

"We are too, honey."

My parents like Dev, although they don't love him like I do. No one loves him like I do since no one knows him like I do, not even the Bastards. I'm the one he let inside his life, his heart. He's made connections with others, real connections,

228

and repaired the ones that he broke or let die... but what's between us is unique.

Dad is waiting for us just outside. He's very handsome in his suit as he offers one arm to me. My mom takes my other arm. I wanted both of them to walk with me down the aisle.

Someone gives the cue to the string quartet and the music begins, low and quiet at first until it swells to fill the air.

"Here we go," Dad says.

The wedding is under a massive tent lit by a thousand glittering lights. It's like the stars are out during the day. As we come to the end of the aisle, everyone stands.

I look past them all to find Dev. When our gazes meet, it's exactly like that moment all those years ago when I saw him outside the garage. It's recognition and attraction and yes, love, only a thousand times deeper because of what we've been through since then.

He's not smiling, which somehow makes him look even more handsome. It's not his blank look either; it's reverence and a joy too deep for mere smiling. His suit is as dark as his hair, the white of his shirt dazzling. He's wearing a tie, which he never does, the same shade of gold as his eyes, only deeper, darker.

I can hardly breathe he looks so good.

And then we're moving down the aisle, Dad and Mom and me. I meet the eyes of several people in the crowd, grinning at all of them.

I see Mark and January first. Mark is holding their daughter Ginny, who's asleep on his shoulder, while January leans against his other shoulder. Mark, who used to be the playboy of Silicon Valley, is deeply content.

Then comes Logan and Callie. Logan's holding Jake's hand and Callie's holding Aurelie's hand, the kids a bridge between them. Their marriage is one of the strongest I know.

Finn and Doc are seated just in front of Callie and Logan. Finn's smiling so hard I think he might bust out laughing at any moment. Doc is in his arms, tucked under his chin so that her blue hair is caught in his beard. Her brother stands next to them, looking very fit. Finn got him into weightlifting apparently.

We take a few more steps, and then I see Grace and Paul. Grace's hands rest on her pregnant belly while Paul's got an arm looped around her shoulder. They both look impossibly elegant, even among the elite of San Francisco.

Elliot and Emily are in the second row from the front, holding hands. While Dev proposed almost immediately after we got together, we wanted to wait until it was safe for these two to come back for the wedding. Emily's something of a national hero now, and her face has been on dozens of newsmagazines. Elliot isn't quite so famous, but we all know he's Emily's rock.

When we reach the altar, everything falls away. Because there's Dev, waiting for me.

He hugs my mother, whispering something in her ear, then shakes hands with Dad. They both go find their seats, leaving the two of us alone in front of everyone.

I reach up, push back the strand of hair that's fallen over his forehead. I kept meaning to remind him to get a haircut before the wedding, but I realize now that would have been a mistake. His hair is perfect like this.

He takes my hands in his, holds tightly. The judge is saying something about love and joining and coming together to celebrate, but I don't hear any of it. There's only Dev and the way he's looking at me, like I'm everything he's ever wanted. Like I'm a dream come true.

I feel the exact same way.

ABOUT THE AUTHOR

Raleigh fell in love with billionaire romance as a teenager thanks to Harlequin Presents. She fell in love with San Francisco in her twenties thanks to how charming the city was. And she fell for a coding genius thanks to how charming *he* was.

Naturally, she had to put all of the things she loved into her romances.

You can find her online at www.raleighdavis.com.